Tony took out ~~~~~ ~~~~~ lifted a small pile of p~~~~~ ~~~~~ into the light of the foy~~~~~ ~~~~~ laid them on the hall table. The grim expression on his face and furious glint in his eyes made a chill race up her spine.

"Tony? What is it?" Erin asked.

Tony turned to one of the police officers. "Call it in. This is a crime scene. We need forensics here stat."

Erin stepped closer for a look at the photographs splayed across the tabletop. Her stomach twisted in knots and her legs threatened to collapse. They were photographs of her.

At the grocery store. Coming out of work. Sitting on the porch. Playing with Jack in the yard. There were even pictures of her at the Easter picnic fundraiser.

And every picture had a black *X* over her face.

DIANE BURKE

is the mother of two grown sons and the grandmother of three wonderful growing-like-weeds grandsons. She has two daughters-in-law that have blessed her by their addition to her family. She lives in Florida, nestled somewhere between the Daytona Beach speedway and the St. Augustine fort, with Cocoa, her golden Lab, and Thea, her border collie. Thea and Cocoa don't know they are dogs, because no one has ever told them. Shhhh.

When she was growing up, her siblings always believed she could "exaggerate" her way through any story and often waited with bated breath to see how events turned out, even though they had been present at most of them. Now she brings those stories to life on the written page.

Her writing has earned her numerous awards, including a Daphne du Maurier Award of Excellence.

She would love to hear from her readers. You can contact her at diane@dianeburkeauthor.com.

MIDNIGHT CALLER
DIANE BURKE

Steeple
Hill®

Published by Steeple Hill Books™

STEEPLE HILL BOOKS

Steeple
Hill®

Recycling programs
for this product may
not exist in your area.

ISBN-13: 978-0-373-44387-1

MIDNIGHT CALLER

www.SteepleHill.com

Printed in U.S.A.

Even when I walk through the darkest valley,
I will not be afraid, for you are close beside me…
—*Psalms* 23:4

To my siblings, Thomas Donahue, Michael Donahue, Cathy Joki, Brian Donahue, Brendan Donahue and Lori Hoskins— each one in their own unique way helped shape me into the person I am today.

To Dan, Claudia, Jeptha, Jesse, Luke, Dave and Esther—the keepers of my heart.

To Sarah McDaniel and Tina James for their encouragement, patience and wisdom—you made this story the best it could be.

To Sergeant Eric Dietrich and retired detective John Foxjohn—who gave generously of their time and wisdom.

To Connie Neumann, author, mentor, friend—at my side from beginning to end. Thanks so much.

To the KOD lethaladies critique groups—both groups helped me shape and grow this story. Thanks doesn't seem good enough.

To Bill Burke—you believed this day would happen long before I dared to hope. I wish you had lived long enough to see it. But somehow I believe you already know. I miss you so very much.

And most of all, to my Lord and Savior, Jesus Christ—my shelter, my strength, my joy. All praise and honor is yours.

ONE

His fingers tapped an angry rhythm against the handle of the scalpel hidden in his pocket. Where was she? He checked his wristwatch for the third time in as many minutes. Her shift had ended thirty minutes ago. She should be standing in that doorway by now.

Alone.

Vulnerable.

A boom of thunder, like cannon fire, shook the ground. A stinging stream of water hit his face, but still he didn't move from beneath the tree. He simply raised his umbrella and continued to stare at the entrance to the hospital.

Finally!

A petite woman in her early thirties paused in the doorway of Florida Memorial and frowned at the weather.

What kept you, sweetheart? What's the matter? Afraid a little rain might hurt you? He chuckled at the irony of his thoughts. He shoved his hand back into his pocket, grasping and releasing the weapon. His pulse quickened. His skin quivered in anticipation.

From a distance, he watched as she rummaged through her tote bag and pulled out a magazine. A grin twisted his lips. *Like that's going to protect you. Like anything could protect you now.*

Eyeing the storm once more, the woman placed the magazine over her head and dashed to the parking lot.

He shadowed her at a discreet distance, not that it would have mattered. She was so busy trying to save herself from the storm, she was oblivious to her true danger.

She fumbled with her keys and dropped them. Seeming to realize the futility of trying to stay dry, she lowered the magazine, scooped up her keys and unlocked her car door. Her blond hair, wet and matted, hugged her skull.

He took out his own keys and slipped into the truck parked behind her blue minivan. Adjusting the rearview mirror, he watched her back out of her parking space. Her brake lights glowed at the stop sign before she signaled and turned into the late-afternoon traffic.

He turned the key in the ignition.

Hurry, little one, this way and that. None of it will matter because death is right behind you.

"I hate cops!" The kitchen door slammed shut behind Erin O'Malley. Seeing her aunt and son sitting at the table, she grinned sheepishly. "Sorry." She deposited the groceries in her arms on the counter.

Aunt Tess chuckled. "Sounds like someone got another speeding ticket."

"Yeah, going forty-five in a thirty-five zone. I'm a genuine NASCAR driver."

"Mommy, it's not nice to say you hate cops," Erin's five-year-old son, Jack, mumbled through a mouthful of cereal. "Cops are the good guys."

Good guys? One of those good guys had raised her, teaching her all she needed to know about secrets, pain and loss. And Jack's dad had been one of those "good guys," too. But it didn't stop him from hightailing it out of their lives when Jack was diagnosed with cerebral palsy. No, thank you very much. She'd had enough of those "good guys" to last a lifetime.

"You've packed so much cereal in your mouth that the pressure has clogged up your ears, little man. Mommy said she ran into some 'great cops.'" She kissed her son's forehead and ruffled his hair. "Besides, what did I tell you about talking with food in your mouth?"

"Oh-kay." Jack gulped and swallowed his last bite. "I'm ready. Let's go."

Erin was daydreaming about a day off and almost didn't hear her son. A day of rest. Puttering around in her garden. Reading a book from her growing to-be-read pile. Maybe even sneaking in a bubble bath. The temptation to indulge herself brought a smile to her lips.

"Now, Jack, I think your mother might be a bit tuckered out." Tess patted his hand. "Why don't you and I have a picnic in the backyard and let your mother get some rest."

Jack turned to face her, his eyes wide. "But, Mommy, you promised."

The urgency in his voice snagged her attention. She blinked and just looked at him while her brain scrambled to get out of daydream mode and process what he said. She remembered now. They'd been planning to attend the annual Wish for the Stars fundraiser and today was the big day.

This year it coincided with the upcoming Easter holiday. Carol Henderson, her best friend and member of the planning committee, told them the opening ceremony included a parade led by the Easter Bunny and more than five thousand eggs hidden away for the hunt. Later, there'd be music, hot dogs, hamburgers, soda and chips. All for a nominal price of admission.

Jack grew more excited as the day approached. His excitement must have stemmed from the thought of having a whole afternoon to play with Amy, Carol's daughter. Best of friends just like their moms, they had fewer play dates due to crazy work schedules now that the hospital was transitioning to the new building.

Or maybe he was excited because he loved picnics.

Either way, Erin had to admit she was looking forward to the event herself. She'd been antsy lately. Feeling unsettled. Wary. And not sure why. Probably because winter had clung longer than normal to Florida this year.

Or maybe she felt unsettled because she hadn't been sleeping well lately because of prank calls throughout the night.

Erin's gaze fell upon the small walker beside her son's chair and her heart clenched. No matter how tired she was or how inviting a relaxing day at home might be she knew she couldn't let her son down. After all, asking to go on an Easter egg hunt wasn't unreasonable. She glanced at her watch. If they hurried, they'd be just in time for the parade.

"Finish your milk and we'll go," Erin said.

Jack reached for his glass and knocked it over.

Erin grabbed a dish towel and started to sop up the liquid.

"I'll get Jack changed," Tess said.

Erin nodded. "Thanks, Tess. Don't know what we'd do without you."

"Never mind that," she said, but blushed beneath the compliment. She shooed Jack toward the bedroom.

Erin glanced at the empty doorway and thought about how lucky she was that Tess had moved in to help after Erin's father, Tess's brother, had died. It had taken years for her father and Erin to reconcile but she had been devastated when he was killed. She didn't think she would have made it through without Tess and her newfound faith to comfort her.

The phone rang.

Lost in thought, the trilling sound startled her. It rang a second time. She stood perfectly still, staring at the instrument like it was a dagger poised to strike. *Please, God, not another one.*

She hugged her arms to her body. Uneasiness crept up her spine. She was surprised she was letting a few anonymous telephone calls make her this jittery. It had to be that boy down the street. He had harassed the neighborhood for days last year until his father discovered what he was doing. He was probably up to his old tricks. She needed to get a hold of herself. And she needed to go have a chat with the boy's dad.

Erin grabbed the phone on the fourth ring.

"Hello."

Silence.

"Hello?"

No reply. She'd answered at least a dozen calls over the past three days, half of them waking her in the middle of the night.

"I know you're there." Erin pressed the phone tightly against her ear. Straining to hear something. Anything. The breathing grew heavier, but still, no one spoke.

"Quit calling here or I'm going to call the police." She slammed the phone in the cradle. Yep, it had to be a bored teenager playing a prank. Absently rubbing her arms, she continued to stare at the instrument. But it didn't *feel* like a prank. She didn't hear muffled giggles on the end of the line. She heard— She didn't know what she heard. She only knew that her instincts blared an inner warning that something was wrong and she had learned through the school of hard knocks to trust those instincts.

"Ready, Mom?" Jack rolled his walker across the room and grinned up at her, wearing his favorite green-striped shirt with the dinosaur logo and a pair of jeans.

Shaking off her anxiety as the result of lack of sleep, she leaned down and hugged him. "You bet. Let's go."

Less than an hour later, while they waited by the side of the parade route, Erin's sense of uneasiness returned. Crazy as it was, she couldn't shake the feeling that someone was watching them. Goose bumps shivered along her arms. Glancing over her shoulder, her eyes roamed the crowd. Children and adults formed two lines up and down the parade route. Some of the parents had brought folding chairs. Others stood. Children sat cross-legged in the grass. A young couple chased a laughing toddler bent on escape.

Nothing sinister. Nothing ominous. Why couldn't she shake this feeling?

Erin recognized many of her coworkers from the hospital. She couldn't identify everyone by name, but she'd passed them in the halls or had ridden with them on an elevator. She waved to the ones she did know and nodded to others. It seemed like half the hospital staff came. Dr. Clark and his family. Shelley from the cafeteria crew. Mr. Peters from housekeeping. Even Lenny, the lab tech, had come. But that was no big surprise. The hospital cosponsored the event and all personnel had been encouraged to buy a ticket.

She turned her head and her eyes lit on her friend. She waved for Carol to join them. Erin banished her anxiety when Carol elbowed her way through the crowd and stood beside her.

"Can you believe this?" Carol asked. "I knew we'd have a crowd, but this is twice as many people as I expected. Times are tough. Money is tight, but it didn't stop folks from reaching into their wallets to buy a ticket for a good cause, did it?"

Carol scooped Amy up into her arms. The child's soft blond curls framed a little round face which held a smiling mouth and the slightly slanted eyes of a three-year-old Down syndrome child.

"You've done a great job, Carol."

"Not just me. The committee worked hard and it looks like it paid off." Music began playing and the excitement of the crowd became palpable. The sound of children's laughter and yells of excitement tinkled in the air like wind chimes.

"The parade's about to begin. Look," Carol said, pointing to her right. "Here comes the Easter Bunny."

He steadied the camera and clicked a picture. Then, he took another. He cursed when people moved in front of him and obstructed his view of her. *Move. All of you. Get out of my way.* He elbowed his way through the crowd until her image filled the camera lens again. *Click.* She threw her head back and laughed. *Click.* She shaded her eyes against the sun while she talked. *Click. Click. Click.*

Her son waited for his mother's attention. The child leaned heavily on the walker, shifting his weight from one leg to another. But his mother was too busy flapping her gums to pay any attention to him. The boy tugged on her shirt. She glanced down, signaled for the child to wait a minute and returned to her conversation. He knew it. He knew he was right about her. She was self-centered and selfish. A rotten excuse for a mother.

He wasn't at all surprised when the boy wandered away. The woman didn't even notice he had gone. A deep hatred flowed through his veins like molten lava. She was like all the other women. Soon he would make her pay. *Click.* First he had to finish the job he started last night. *Click.* She'd pay, all right. *Click. Click.* She deserved to die.

* * *

The sun beat down without mercy as Tony Marino looked out over the crowd from his vantage point on top of the picnic table. Not even a hint of a breeze. This kind of weather you expected in August in Florida not April. *Remember spring, Lord? Supposed to be warm and balmy, not hot and sticky.* But it was hot. Miserably hot. And he wasn't any closer to finding a lead on this case.

He wanted to curse so badly his lips twitched. Five years ago when Tony had found the Lord and decided to mend his ways, cursing seemed the easiest vice to attack first. He was wrong. As a detective for the Volusia County sheriff's office cursing had been a natural part of his daily conversation. No different than any other word. He started out promising himself to say a prayer and put a dollar in a jar each time he uttered a curse word. When his prayers took hours and his jar collected enough money to buy a small car, he knew it was going to be more difficult than he first believed.

But he succeeded.

Not one errant word in five years.

Until today.

Sweat rolled down the back of his neck and beaded on his forehead. All he could think about was the case. He wanted to call his partner. See if there were any new leads. He wanted to get back to the files on his desk. Maybe he'd missed something. He wanted to be anywhere but here. What a colossal waste of his time, babysitting a stupid rabbit.

He glanced at the cage resting beside him. The rabbit didn't look hot or uncomfortable despite the crazy multicolored cape tied to its body. It just chomped away on a carrot totally oblivious to the world. Lucky rabbit.

He couldn't believe he'd been roped into this job in the first place. Carrying the "Easter Bunny" at the head of the parade and officiating at the opening of the Easter egg hunt. He knew the captain liked his men to volunteer in the community. Winters had played Santa for the kids in the hospital. Garcia, dressed as a super hero, had toured the schools and talked about the danger of drugs. But when his number had come up on the volunteer list, what did Sarge assign him? Easter Bunny duty at the fundraiser for the Wish for the Stars Foundation. Great foundation. Fulfilled dreams for sick children. Good for the kids. The pits for him.

Tony had agreed to do it not just because it was his turn. Or because it was for a charity he deeply believed in. But last night another woman had gone missing. He planned to mingle with the crowd. Keep his ears open to idle conversations. Keep his eyes open for anything out of the ordinary. Because something was very much out of the ordinary. A monster had invaded their peaceful community. They'd already discovered two bodies and now a third woman was missing.

Tony scanned the crowd for the hundredth time. It looked like a Norman Rockwell painting and he smiled in spite of himself. Children of all ages, shapes and sizes covered the grounds like ants at a picnic. The organizers had done a good job of dividing the kids not just by age group, but also by disability. Children in wheelchairs were accompanied by volunteers to help them hunt and many of them picked up their own eggs using long-handled reachers.

His eyes slid over the adults. Mothers helped their children. Fathers snapped pictures. Was one of them a murderer? Experience had taught him that the most frightening serial killers were the ones who could blend easily into the normal thread of life. The neighbor waving hello as he mowed the grass. The guy delivering the morning paper. The man walking his dog.

Now a killer was here in his community, kidnapping and brutally killing women. Tony was determined to find him.

The smell of charcoaled hamburgers wafted across the lawn. His stomach growled in response. He hadn't had more than a doughnut and coffee for breakfast. He was more than ready to relinquish his furry charge. The rabbit could go back to doing whatever rabbits do and he could grab a burger and head back to the department.

In his peripheral vision, he caught a glimpse of movement. He turned his head. A boy, five maybe six years old, approached. Tony groaned. Just what he needed. A kid coming to see the rabbit. He watched the child push the walker with the speed and determination of a little man on a mission. Tony grinned. The boy reminded him of himself when he'd been that age. Full of curiosity and excess energy. He'd been a real handful for his single mom. To this day he never knew how she managed to raise him all on her own.

An unruly mass of red hair sprouted from the kid's head. He looked like a cartoon character who had stuck his finger into an electric socket. In the distance, a woman with bouncing auburn curls was in hot pursuit. Must be the mother.

The child pushed the walker up to the table and stared into the cage.

The boy's serious expression intrigued Tony. "Why aren't you hunting eggs with the other kids?"

"He's not real, is he?" The boy's frown deepened.

Tony glanced at the rabbit and shrugged. "Looks real to me."

"There's no such thing as an Easter Bunny. It's all pretend." The boy's shoulders slumped and his lower lip jutted out.

"Jack, don't bother the man." The mother had caught up. Winded from her race to catch up with her son, her words came in short gasps. Her eyes held the remnants of fear probably from realizing he had wandered away. "Why did you leave without telling me?" She lowered her voice to a whisper meant for her son. "You know the rule about talking to strangers."

A blond-haired woman, her arms wrapped around a child with Down syndrome, appeared behind them. "Don't be too hard on him, Erin. We were talking. It was probably hard to resist coming to see the Easter Bunny. Right, Jack?"

Jack looked at Tony. "Do kids really get wishes? Or is that pretend, too?"

"Why? Do you have a wish?" Tony asked.

The boy nodded. "I've been wishing and praying every night and I didn't know how God was going to help me. But I heard Mom and Aunt Carol talking. She said that kids get to make a wish and sometimes that wish comes true. Since you're in charge of the Easter Bunny, I figure God wants me to ask you."

"Jack." The mom placed her hand on the boy's shoulder. "What are you talking about? What wish?"

"Yes, Jack," Tony said with a grin. "What is this wish that's so big you've been praying about it?"

"I need a dad."

"Jack!" The mother coughed and sputtered. Her friend gasped and then burst into laughter.

"Not a real dad," Jack spoke faster. "A pretend dad would be fine. But I need him by eight o'clock next Saturday."

"Eight o'clock?" Tony, just as surprised as the mother, could only echo the boy's words.

Jack's head bobbed up and down. "Mrs. Meltzer at Kidz Club says it doesn't have to be a real dad. It can be a stepdad or an uncle or a grandfather or even a big brother. That's what you need to ride the boys' bus to Disney World. But I don't have any of those things. It's just me, my mom and Aunt Tess. I really want to go on that bus."

The mother's face and throat flushed with color. She was an attractive woman. Slender. Medium height. Auburn hair. Green eyes. An appealing package. The woman seemed to be struggling to find something appropriate to say. "Jack," was the only word she managed to whisper.

"Moms get to go. And sisters, too," the boy continued. "But they have to ride on the second bus. Only the guys get to ride the first bus. Mom's going with me. But if I don't get a pretend dad, I won't be able to ride the first bus with the rest of the guys. I don't want to ride the girls' bus."

"Jack Patrick O'Malley, you stop it right this minute."

A smile tugged at the edges of Tony's mouth. Obviously, the mother had overcome her embarrassment and slid right on into mad-as-all-get-out.

"I don't want to be different from the other kids," Jack said, ignoring his mother's outburst. "My legs don't work right. I can't play with the other kids at recess. I have to use this stupid walker all the time. I want to go on the boys' bus. I want to be just like everybody else even if it's only for one day. Can you do it? Can you get me a pretend dad for Saturday?"

Tony drew in a deep breath.

Lord, how am I supposed to handle this? Couldn't he have wished for a train set or an action figure? No, he had to hit me in the gut with this. Please, Father, give me the right words.

"That's a pretty big order." He looked into the expectant, freckled face staring up at him and, again, saw himself as a boy. Although too young to have any real memories of his police officer father who had been killed in the line of duty, he remembered only too well the pain of growing up without a dad.

Tony's chest constricted when he saw the trust and hope reflected in the boy's eyes. "Some things are tough, Jack, even for me," he said gently. "But I'll see what the Easter bunny and I can do. Why don't you go with your aunt?" He pointed toward the refreshments. "I need to talk with your mom."

Carol, still chuckling, led Jack and Amy away.

Erin watched the man get down from the table and stretch to his full six-foot-two height. He was tall, dark and lethally handsome. She wished the ground would open up and swallow her. "I'm so sorry," she said. "When he said he had a wish, I thought he would ask for a new toy or a video game. I don't know what to say."

Her discomfort deepened when with an athletic grace he covered the distance between them in seconds. His T-shirt strained against his muscular arms and chest. A pleasant masculine scent teased her nostrils and Erin squelched a sudden, irrational urge to move closer for a deeper whiff. But it was his eyes that moved her. Deep, dark, chocolate eyes lit with amusement and a hint of something else. Empathy?

Empathy she appreciated. Sympathy she didn't need from anyone.

"Relax," he said. "Don't you know? I hang out with the Easter Bunny. Who knows better than me the surprising things that slip out of the mouths of kids?" He offered his hand. "I'm Tony Marino."

His grip was firm and strong.

"Erin O'Malley."

He released her hand and gestured for her to wait. He pulled a wallet from his back pocket, withdrew a business card and handed it to her.

"I work for the Sheriff's Department."

"You're a cop?" *What else could go wrong today?*

Tony nodded. "A detective." His eyes held a warmth and compassion that made his next words easier to hear. "I'd like to volunteer to accompany Jack on the boys' bus."

This tall, muscular man with a giving heart and a voice like hot, southern honey made Erin stand up and take notice despite his bad taste in permanent employment.

He nodded toward the business card. "You can verify my credentials before Saturday, ma'am."

She refrained from answering and tried to make sense of her ridiculous, and completely unexpected, attraction to him. Just the word *cop* usually worked like a bucket of ice-cold water. And the fact that he was a member of the untrustworthy male species normally cinched the deal.

"Why would you want to ride the bus with my son?" she asked.

"That's what today is all about, isn't it? Granting wishes to kids?" He leaned close. His breath fanned her cheek and he whispered in her ear as if they shared a secret all their own. "I know from personal experience what it feels like to grow up without a dad. I know what it would mean to your son to ride the bus with the other boys."

"I…I…" A multitude of emotions bombarded Erin. Surprise. Embarrassment. Curiosity. Goose bumps danced along her arms when those chocolate eyes locked with hers. She glanced at the card in her hand and, for once, was speechless.

"Don't answer now," Tony said. "Just think about it and let me know." With a wink and a wave, he picked up the rabbit cage and left.

Erin was touched by the man's kindness. Helping out for the Wish for the Stars fundraiser. Volunteering to ride the bus with her son. But she had promised herself not to get involved again with *any* man, especially a cop. Men lie and men leave.

After church, Tony entered the station. He had prayed hard at the service that morning that the Lord would provide a lead, a direction, something to help them find the missing woman before she became the next victim. He walked past the bull pen and headed toward the lockers. His senses heightened. Something wasn't right. Knowing how he hated Easter duty, the guys had been ribbing him all week. Now that he had actually done the deed not a sound came from the peanut gallery.

He nodded to Richard Spence and Brad Winters as he passed their desks. They looked up, nodded and returned to work. *Thank You, Lord. It's about time they moved on to something else. They're good detectives, but sometimes they act like jerks.*

Tony crossed the break room and opened his locker. A flood of rocks…no, not rocks…eggs…plastic eggs bounced off his head, his shoulders and rolled over his feet. Loud, raucous laughter sounded behind him. Tony saw Spence, Winters and a half-dozen other guys squeezed into the doorway, straining to get a bird's-eye view.

"Funny, guys. Real funny." Tony had to admit it was a pretty good prank. He chuckled, kicked a path through the eggs, and elbowed his way past the gawking men to his desk. His backside barely hit his chair when a loud, commanding voice caught his attention.

"Marino, don't get comfortable. Spence. Winters. In my office." Sergeant Greene hollered from his office doorway. Expecting to be chastised for the egg incident, they filed into the room like guilty schoolchildren and flopped into the chairs in front of the desk.

The sergeant slid a manila folder across the desk. "Here's the latest information on our missing woman. Now we have a face to go with the name."

Tony picked up the folder, flipped it open and looked at the picture inside. She was an average, pleasant-looking woman. Brown hair. Brown eyes. Her smile warm and generous.

"Cynthia Mayors is thirty-one, married and has two children under the age of eight," Greene said. "Her husband was notified this morning and is making arrangements to fly home from Iraq as soon as possible. Meantime, Child Protective Services has been called in to care for the kids."

Frick and Frack, otherwise known as Spence and Winters, respectively, leaned sideways stealing a glance at the picture. Spence squinted his eyes and looked closer. "She probably ran off with her boyfriend."

"Didn't you hear?" Winters asked. "He said she's married, stupid."

"Since when does that mean anything? Just because she's married doesn't mean she doesn't have a boyfriend," insisted Spence. "Matter of fact, I'm sure of it. Look at that picture. She's grinning from ear to ear. You only see grins like that when everything is new, exciting, and reality hasn't hit you over the head with a cast iron pot. Don't see married folk grinning like that as the years add up."

"Speak for yourself. You wouldn't know a good marriage if you fell over it. The ink's not even dry on your divorce papers yet. What divorce is it, anyway? Three? Four?" Winters brushed a piece of lint from his impeccably ironed trousers. "I'm married fifteen years this May and if you took a photo of me today, I'd be grinning up a storm."

"Really? You're sitting there grinning? Then I'm thinking I need glasses 'cause the only thing I see when I look at you is the same old sourpuss who walks around here all day like his shoes are too tight." Spence looked pleased with himself for the comeback.

"Enough," the sergeant yelled. "Can we get back to the matter at hand and leave the school yard antics outside?"

Spence and Winters glared at each other.

Bringing the conversation back to business, Tony said, "I didn't see or hear anything out of the ordinary at the picnic yesterday, Sarge. I'd bet no one even knows she's missing. When was she last seen?"

"Friday. A couple of the nurses report she left right after the three o'clock shift change. She never arrived home. The babysitter called it in late Friday night."

"Has anyone mentioned anything that might help us out?" Winters asked. "Trouble at home? Trouble on the job? Anybody hanging around or bothering her?"

"As you know, we've just begun the investigation," Sarge said. "So far we know her husband's in Iraq. She talks about her family a lot, especially her kids. Carried umpteen photos in her purse and took the time to show them every chance she had. Other than her husband being away, everything seemed good on the home front. From what I've heard, she's well-liked by her peers. As far as a stalker, no one noticed anyone suspicious hanging around."

Sergeant Greene leaned back in his chair. A scowl twisted his features. "The particulars of her disappearance match those of the other two women we've lost."

Winters said, "How do you figure, Sarge? Both our prior victims were single. This one's married."

"And both our other ladies are dead," Spence said.

"That's why we've got to move on this pronto, gentlemen," Sarge replied. "All three women seem to have disappeared into thin air. No witnesses. No signs of struggle. Two of the women left their jobs and never arrived home. The third woman left her home for an appointment and never arrived. That's enough to tie them together for me."

The sergeant tossed his chewed yellow pencil on the table. "It's worth a hard look. If there's a connection between

Cynthia Mayors and the other two victims, I want to know it before she becomes victim number three. This isn't New York or Chicago. If a woman's body shows up here, we're probably looking at a domestic dispute, a drug overdose or a bar pickup gone bad. Two women disappear in this community and then turn up dead? That raises the hair on the back of my neck. A third woman vanishes? I gotta tell you I'm wondering if Ted Bundy's younger brother just moved to town."

"We hear you, Sarge. We'll get on it right away," said Winters.

Tony picked up the folder and carried it back to his desk. Yesterday's picnic had been a waste of his time. He should have been out with the other men canvassing the neighborhood, conducting interviews.

The image of a freckle-faced boy and a mom with auburn hair popped into his mind. He had to admit it hadn't been a total waste of time. He might have the chance to do something special for a handicapped kid. That made him feel good.

He loved kids but decided never to have a family of his own. Choosing to be a cop was a twenty-four-hour, seven-day-a-week, dangerous job. He didn't want to subject a child to the possibility of growing up without a father. Been there, knew that pain. So he fed the occasional paternal urge with his sister's kids or helped out with the church youth group.

Besides, what kind of father would he be? He'd never had a role model. Just like that kid he'd met today. No uncles. Not even an older brother. His mom didn't bring dates home to meet him 'til his late teens. It had been just him, his mom and his sister. What if he didn't measure up? He saw the results of bad parenting every day on his job. Nope. No kids for him.

Tony dragged his hand over his face. He needed to buckle down and work. But on what? They didn't have one lead that hadn't been investigated. As much as it sickened him, he had to acknowledge they'd hit a brick wall and couldn't do another thing but retrace their steps until the killer made another move.

He flipped open the folder and studied the picture. This woman was somebody's wife, somebody's mother, somebody's friend. Experience told him she was probably already dead. Sarge was right. Three was a very unsettling number.

TWO

Erin tugged the business card out of her pocket.

"I see you still haven't thrown that away." Tess plopped her ample girth onto a nearby kitchen chair. "Must be you are at least considering the lad's offer." The older woman squinted. "What are you doing in here, anyway? Cleaning the kitchen is my job."

"I thought I'd give you a hand."

"You know what they say about two cooks in a kitchen…"

Erin smiled. Tess was notorious for spouting the first line of famous sayings and never finishing them. One of these days, she was going to put her on the spot and see if she even knew the other halves of those sayings.

"So?" Her aunt peered across eyeglasses riding low on her nose and waited.

"I have no intention of taking his offer seriously."

"Is that so?" Tess pretended to brush nonexisting crumbs off the table into her upturned palm. "Even though you went through the trouble to find out he is, indeed, an honorable law enforcement officer?"

Erin ignored her.

"Even though Jack has his heart set on riding the boys' bus? Even though the gentleman was nice enough to offer to ride with him? You're just not going to do it. Makes sense to me. Sure it does."

Erin sighed. "You don't understand. I can't ask a total stranger to play Jack's dad. It's humiliating."

"First of all, lass, he's not a stranger. He's a police officer from our very own community who has a kind heart for a handicapped boy. And you're not asking him to play Jack's dad. Just to accompany him on the bus. Besides, he volunteered."

"We've been over this a hundred times. No. Now that's the end of it."

"Harrumph. That's stubbornness and pride speaking."

"Well, it must be an inherited trait." She shot Tess her best "don't go there" glare.

The older woman pushed back her chair and stood. "Maybe you ought to pray on it. I know Jack's been praying every night. Did you ever stop to think that maybe the good Lord put this police officer in your path as an answer to Jack's prayers?"

Silence stretched between them.

"I'm going to check on the boy. It's obvious I'm talking to a brick wall in here."

Erin shook her head. What was she going to do with Tess? The sixty-five-year-old had a bad habit of pushing too hard in things that were just none of her business and Erin hadn't found a loving way to discourage the meddling.

Walking over to the trash, she tossed the card in the bin. *There. That's where you belong. You've caused enough trouble in this house.* She stared for several minutes at the small white rectangle lying atop discarded lettuce. Instead of a business card, she saw dark eyes framed by crinkled smile lines. She felt the soft caress of his breath against her skin. She smelled the musky, masculine scent of him.

Shaking her head to rid herself of those nonproductive thoughts another image slipped into her consciousness, the pleading eyes of her son. Before she could change her mind, she snatched the card back up, swiped it on the leg of her jeans to wipe off any lettuce residue and shoved it back into her pocket.

Erin had finished sweeping the floor when Tess reentered the room. "Everything, okay?"

Tess chuckled. "The lad's built a small city in the living room with those plastic blocks. Maybe he'll be an architect when he grows up."

Before she could respond, the phone rang. She snatched up the receiver. "Hello?" Erin paused for several seconds before repeating her greeting. "Hello, is anybody there?" She strained to listen and was certain she heard breathing. Someone was there. Why didn't they answer? Her mouth twisted in a frown and she hung up.

"Who was it?" Tess asked.

"Nobody. Probably a wrong number."

"Funny, they can't dial the number they want, but they can remember our number long enough to call it a dozen times by mistake."

Erin poured herself a mug of freshly brewed coffee and joined her aunt at the kitchen table. "Maybe it's a telemarketer. These days a computer dials the number and connects to a salesperson only after you answer. It takes a bit for the connection to go through."

"Uh-huh." Tess pushed her bifocals down her nose and stared intently at her niece. "And I suppose you're wearing your worry face because you're afraid you might be missin' the sale of a lifetime?"

Erin chuckled and sipped her coffee.

"I might be getting a little deaf, lass, but I'm not blind.

Someone's been calling this house at odd hours for the past four days and I never see you talking to anyone. What's going on?"

Erin shrugged. "Honestly, Tess, I haven't a clue. I answer. They don't. End of story."

"Don't tell me 'end of story.' Did you write down the number from your caller ID?"

"There isn't one. It just reads unknown name, unknown number."

"You need to find out who it is."

She patted the older woman's hand. "Don't get in a dither. It's just some teenagers playing a prank. They'll get tired and move on to someone else." She carried her empty mug to the sink.

"Erin O'Malley, you sit back down here and listen to me."

Erin, surprised at her aunt's tone of voice, did as she was told.

"We're not livin' in the world I grew up in." Tess waggled a finger at her. "Used to be you left your doors unlocked. You knew your neighbors and everybody watched out for everybody else. Today it's a world of strangers. Nobody even takes the time to know the person livin' right next door. There are more bad guys and less of a way to know who the bad guys are until it's too late."

The animation and emotion in her aunt's face surprised Erin. "I never knew you had such strong feelings about this."

"Why shouldn't I? Age blesses one with wisdom, lass. We are two single women living alone with a handicapped child to protect. You need to be more concerned when something strange happens. How can you protect yourself, or us, if you don't keep your eyes open to what's going on around you? And what's going on around you right now isn't right. You need to fix it."

"And how am I supposed to do that?" Erin asked, suddenly

suspicious of her aunt's true motives. "Call a cop? Or did you have a particular detective in mind?"

"I don't know what you're talking about." Tess ducked her head.

Erin almost laughed out loud at the expression on her aunt's face when she realized her ploy hadn't worked.

"Shame on you for trying to scare me," Erin said.

"I'm speakin' the truth," Tess insisted. "If you used that brain of yours, you'd be smart enough to be scared." Tess carried her own empty mug to the sink. "I don't see how it could hurt to ask the detective's advice. He's expecting you to call him anyway. So do it." She glanced over her shoulder. "And just so you know, I meant every word I said."

"You're right. I need to report the calls," Erin said. "I would have called the police before now, but I really thought it was Billy Sanders. Remember last year when he harassed everybody in the neighborhood for days with heavy breathing and giggles?"

Tess nodded as she started washing her cup. "That boy needed a good swift kick in his…"

"Anyway," Erin said. "I thought he was doing it again, so I went over to see his dad this morning."

"Really? How'd that go?"

"It's not Billy. His dad tells me the boy has straightened out. Joined a church youth group. Matter of fact, he was away this past weekend at a Christian teen camp."

"Good for him," Tess said. "So what are you going to do about the calls?"

Erin crossed the room and wrapped her arms around her aunt's back, resting her cheek against the back of her head. "I am going to call that 'fine, young detective' you keep pushing down my throat. But you better know, old woman, that I'm on to you and your sneaky ways. I already made up my mind to call the detective. Calls or no calls. I want Jack to ride the bus with the boys."

Tess squealed, turned around and pulled Erin to her despite the soap suds on her hands. "I knew you'd come to your senses. It just takes time for reasonable thoughts to get through your thick, Irish skull."

"I love you, too, Tess."

Tony clenched his teeth so hard his jaw hurt. Ever since he got the call about a corpse discarded in the tall grass by the Tomoka River, he had been dreading this moment. He nodded to Winters and Spence, who had just pulled up. Telltale yellow tape roped off the crime scene. The forensics team was already at work, taking pictures of the body and carefully gathering evidence.

"Hey, Keith." Tony acknowledged the motorcycle cop who had been first on the scene. "What do we have?" Spence and Winters drew up behind him.

"I was heading north on Airport Road when these two kids ran out of the woods, screaming to high heaven and white as sheets. This park has a reputation as a good fishing spot. Seems they got more than they expected. They went into the brush close to the river and, literally, fell over the corpse." Keith nodded toward the boys. "I got them calmed down. They're waiting over there for their parents to pick them up."

Two boys, about eleven or twelve, stole glances in their direction. The shuffling of their feet and the slight green tinge to their skin attested to the fact they wanted to be as far away from the park as possible.

Winters said, "We've got this," and he and Spence headed toward the boys.

Tony ducked under the yellow tape and gingerly approached the medical examiner.

"Hi, Sally." It never ceased to surprise him how a sweet, grandmotherly looking woman would choose to spend her days surrounded by corpses. Go figure.

"Tony."

"What can you tell me?" He squatted beside her.

"Not much yet. Looks like she was killed elsewhere and dumped here. I'll have more specifics for you after I get the body back to the morgue. She fought back. Should get some good DNA samples from under her nails."

Tony glanced at the corpse and knew two things instantly. The body's injuries matched the visible injuries of the other two corpses. And Cynthia Mayors, the woman who had disappeared from the hospital after her Friday shift, was no longer missing.

Several hours later Tony trudged into the office, tired, hungry and with only one thing on his mind: finishing his report and going home.

"Hey, Tony," the desk clerk yelled. "A woman called a couple of hours ago. Left her name and number. Said something about meeting you at the Easter picnic and wanted to talk to you about a problem she's having."

As the clerk's voice rang through the room, Tony grimaced. He glanced at his fellow officers. Here we go. Round three for pranks and jokes. But right now he didn't care. He had hoped she'd call. He didn't like to think she would let her kid down. He took the message from the clerk and headed back to his desk. At least he'd be able to make one little boy's life a little happier. He wished he could have been in time to save Cynthia Mayors's children from the world of hurt he just delivered to them.

* * *

"I'll get it!" Tess's voice drifted down the hallway after the doorbell rang.

Erin retested the water temperature for Jack's bath, then stepped aside. Jack held on to the safety rail and lowered himself onto the nonskid mat. Erin placed clean pajamas and a towel on the toilet seat cover and made sure the walker was placed safely within reach. "I'll have hot chocolate waiting for you when you're done."

Jack, already covered head to toe with soap bubbles, grinned at his mother. "With whipped cream and marshmallows, please. And can I have one of those chocolate chip cookies you hide over the 'frigerator?"

Erin chuckled. "We'll see. Make sure you clean behind your ears."

She walked down the hall and entered the kitchen. "Who was at the—" A rush of pleasure raced through her body at the sight of the man standing beside her aunt. Dressed in a dark gray suit, white shirt and patterned tie, he was even more handsome than when she'd seen him at the park. And those eyes—should be a crime walking around looking so good.

"Hi. Remember me? I didn't bring my rabbit with me. Hope you don't mind," he said.

Her aunt chuckled and busied herself wiping the counter.

"Of course, I remember you, Detective Marino. Please, sit down. Make yourself comfortable."

"Call me Tony." He slipped off his jacket and loosened his tie. "Hope you don't mind. It's been a long day."

"Not at all. I know how you feel. The ER can be stressful at times, too."

"You work at the hospital?" Tony raised an eyebrow and wondered if she knew Cynthia Mayors.

"I'm a nurse in the emergency room," she said with a nod.

"Would you be likin' a spot of coffee, lad?" Tess asked.

Tony acknowledged her. "That I would, ma'am."

"Call me Tess. You've already met my niece, Erin."

Tony extended his hand to Erin. He smiled broadly, his teeth even and white against his tanned skin. "Nice to meet you again, Ms. Erin O'Malley."

There it was. Gorgeous smile. Eyes so captivating it was difficult to look away. Because of her instant attraction to him, Erin expected the familiar goose bumps when her hand slid into his grasp, but she wasn't prepared for this strong pull of emotion and found it surprising. Even a bit confusing. What was the matter with her? He was a cop, remember? Cop, as in don't-even-think-about-it cop. Not to mention the fact that he was a hunk. In her experience the words *male* and *hunk* in the same sentence always spelled trouble, always caused pain.

Tony released her hand. His smile reached his eyes, tiny lines crinkling at the corners just as she remembered.

"I'm glad you called. What time do you want me to pick the two of you up?"

"I…I'm not sure," she stammered. "The bus leaves at eight-thirty."

"I'll be here at seven-thirty. That should give us plenty of time to load anything Jack needs and get there with time to spare."

"Sounds good to me," Tess answered for Erin and placed mugs in the middle of the table. She picked one up and handed it to Tony. "See if this nonalcoholic Irish coffee doesn't cure what ails you."

"Nonalcoholic Irish coffee? Isn't that an oxymoron?" Tony lifted the cup and sipped the dark liquid. Feigning an Irish brogue, he said, "I just had meself a drop of pure magic."

Tess blushed like a schoolgirl.

Erin chuckled. *This guy can charm the socks off of anybody.* When the phone rang, she gestured for her aunt to remain sitting and got up to answer it.

"Hello?" The soft rumble of conversation from the table drifted toward her and made it difficult to hear. She strained to listen for a voice on the line. "Hello?" The silence continued and an insidious trickle of fear knotted her stomach. She slammed down the phone.

Erin knew Tony had noticed the trembling in her hands when she rejoined them at the table and, ashamed of herself for being so easily scared, she folded them on her lap. Feeling the need to explain, she shrugged and said, "Heavy breathing. Hang-ups. Nothing to get upset about."

"How long have you been getting these calls?" Tony asked.

"Since Thursday."

"How often?"

"Hard to say. No set times or frequency."

"Except at night," Tess interrupted. "He's been calling five, maybe six, times a night. No one in this house has had a solid night's sleep in days."

"Have you reported it to the police?" Tony asked.

"Erin has a thing about police. She hates cops. Didn't she tell you?" Tess ducked the censoring look from Erin.

Tony's lips twitched. He seemed to be struggling not to grin. "Hate cops, do you? Well, you're either a convicted felon who's done hard time or a lead-foot driver with multiple tickets. Which one is it? My nickel is on lead foot."

Tess laughed out loud. "See, lass. They don't call him a detective for nothing."

"About those calls?" Tony's eyes held concern and kindness.

"I filed a complaint earlier today," Erin assured both of them.

"The best bet is to let your answering machine screen your

calls," Tony continued. "Pranksters won't call for long if their calls are never answered. I don't think they have as much fun heavy breathing into a recorder."

Tess chuckled.

"I think I'm going to change my number and let the answering machine screen the calls," Erin said.

"Wow, hitting them with heavy artillery. They must have scared you a little more than you're willing to admit," Tony said.

She stared into his eyes. Her silence communicated how right he was.

A young boy's voice filled the air. "I'm ready for my hot chocolate and cookies."

All three adults turned when Jack entered the room. Erin and Tony stood to greet him.

The boy, his wet hair plastered to his skull and still dripping on his blue and green dinosaur pajamas, scooted his walker up to the table. "Hi. You're the man from the park. What are you doing here?"

Erin's eyes met Tony's and a grateful smile graced her lips. "He's giving you your wish, Jack. He's going to be your dad-for-a-day."

THREE

Erin's breath caught in her throat. Her eyes burned. *I will not cry. I won't.* She watched from across the parking lot as Tony and Jack inched their way toward the front of the bus line. It had never been more evident to her than now that she couldn't be everything her son needed. He needed a dad in his life. A dad she had been unable and unwilling to provide. Sadness threatened to overwhelm her. A lone tear escaped and slid down her cheek.

Tony paused before boarding the bus and looked over his shoulder. His eyes locked with hers. He winked, just as he had when they met, sending her a silent assurance that he understood and everything was going to be okay. Then, he lifted Jack to carry him up the steps.

Erin shook her head when she looked at Jack. His cowlicks stood at attention no matter how hard she had tried to gel, mousse and spray them into place. But it was Jack's grin, so wide it barely fit his face, that clenched her heart.

"Bye, Mom," he yelled, waving furiously. His contagious excitement made Erin bounce and wave in return despite the tears that stung her eyes. Her baby was growing up.

From the second they had passed through the turnstiles, Erin had understood why they named it the Magic Kingdom—from the quaint gift shops, the incomparable anima-tronic rides, the fireworks behind Cinderella's castle and the parade down Main Street. The day had been long but exciting and memorable. Tony had been great with Jack. Never losing his patience with the ever-talking, constantly-in-motion boy as they waited in lines or made their way through the crowds. It had been more than Erin expected, much more. For just today, she had allowed herself to pretend they were a family and realized that Jack wasn't the only one who missed having a male figure in their lives.

Tony elbowed his way through the restaurant. "Where do kids get their energy?" he asked as he placed their trays on the table.

Erin helped Jack position his wheelchair and then slid on the bench beside Tony. "He doesn't look energetic now."

Jack, stuffing chicken fingers and fries into his mouth, looked like he could fall asleep chewing. His eyes were heavy and even the din of people talking and bustling past their table didn't faze him.

Erin's legs throbbed and muscles she didn't even know she owned screamed in protest from the hours they had spent racing from one side of the park to the other, not wanting to miss a single thing. She leaned down and rubbed the painful knot in the back of her calf.

"You okay?" Tony asked, nodding his head at her calf. "I can get rid of that cramp for you."

"No, thanks. It's okay."

"Look, trust me."

Trust him? He had no idea how impossible that would be.

"Pull your toes toward your nose. It releases the cramp. When you get home, massage your calf and put a warm compress on the muscles. It should help."

She pulled her toes upward and the seizing pain subsided.

He hid his grin at the surprised look on her face.

"So how do you know so much about leg cramps, Detective?"

Tony shrugged. "Played football in college. Dealt with a couple dozen of them."

She smiled up at him and the bright sparkle of her green eyes stole his breath away. Wispy red curls framed her oval face, cascading in waves over her shoulders and down her back. Full, rosy lips drew his attention. To his surprise he found himself wondering what they'd feel like pressed against his own.

Tony gave himself a mental shake. He was here to do a favor for a boy. Nothing more. He had no time in his schedule or a place in his life for a woman—and most definitely not a single mom with a kid. He needed a distraction and he needed it now. When he glanced across the table, he laughed out loud. Jack, his head propped on his elbow, his mouth hanging open, was sound asleep.

"Looks like Jack's down for the count." Tony grinned. "I thought if he didn't wind down soon, I'd be the one sitting in that wheelchair with him on my lap."

Erin laughed and the delicate, musical sound made him think of wind chimes in a gentle breeze.

"Maybe we ought to call it a day and head back toward the buses. What do you say?" Tony asked.

"My thoughts exactly." She gathered the empty food containers and stacked them on her tray.

Tony didn't want to be but he was drawn to her. Despite his internal alarms telling him to run to the nearest exit. Despite the knowledge that he had nothing he could offer her. This type of woman wanted commitment, permanence. Two words not in his vocabulary.

Yet she intrigued him. She was an enigma. Vulnerable yet strong. Feminine yet fiercely independent. He found the combination intoxicating. He slid his arm around the back of her chair and lifted the edge of her jade silk scarf, letting the delicate fabric slide through his fingers. "This color looks good on you, brings out the color of your eyes."

"Thank you." Her words came out in a husky whisper. Her pulse drummed against the slenderness of her throat. Erin stood and began clearing the table. "Jack had a wonderful day," she said, keeping her eyes averted and her head down. "I don't know how to repay you."

"How about dinner Friday night?" Tony winced the second the words flew out of his mouth.

Erin almost spilled the tray. She set it back down, took a deep breath and faced him. "Nothing personal, Tony. You're a great guy."

Tony didn't know whether to breathe a sigh of relief or be offended.

"Ouch," he said. "Men know those words are the kiss of death."

"You've been really good to Jack…and to me," Erin said. "But I'm not looking for a relationship right now. And even if I was…which I'm definitely not…I have an ironclad rule. I don't date cops."

"Rules are meant to be broken," Tony replied.

Wasn't that the truth? Wasn't he breaking his own ironclad rule to avoid all women with strings attached? No one had more strings than a single mom. He cocked his head and studied her. "A man must have hurt you deeply." *Maybe that was what pulled him. Just his protective instincts rising up. He could deal with that.* Before she could answer, he said, "It doesn't matter. I'm not asking you for a date."

She arched an eyebrow. "Dinner Friday night is not a date?"

"Nope. It's another opportunity for you to shower me

with thanks for a job well done. It's a chance for me to talk about myself to a captive audience. It's even an opportunity to discuss world events and the weather. But it certainly isn't a date."

His lopsided grin almost broke her reserve. She ducked her head so she didn't have to look into those gorgeous brown eyes. She liked this guy. And she didn't want to.

She carried the tray to the trash. Lost in thought, she didn't notice a person trying to squeeze past until it was too late. He slammed into her with the force and speed of a defensive football player. Making a frantic grab for the nearest post to break her fall, she glanced over her shoulder. The man not only hadn't slowed down, he had already disappeared. Steadying herself, she vowed to pay closer attention to her surroundings and keep her mind off of Tony before she got plowed over.

When she returned to their table, Tony's silence made her think he had accepted her answer. Erin bent down to gently wake Jack, but before she did, she stole a glance in Tony's direction. When their eyes met, he did the only thing he could have done to stop her dead in her tracks. He winked.

"He did what?" Carol asked as they sat together behind the nurse's desk in the emergency room.

Erin chuckled. "The egotistical, know-it-all winked at me."

"Are you going to go out with him Friday night?"

"No. He can wink all he wants. A rule is a rule."

Carol finished writing her nurse's note. "The nerve of the man. Well, that's it, then. You have to kill him. And there's not a jury in the world that would convict you." She leaned over Erin's chair and stage-whispered in her ear, "Because they would be too busy finding you certifiably insane."

"Ms. Erin?" Lenny Richards, one of the hospital phlebotomists, interrupted their conversation. "I'm headed to the lab. Call me if you need me."

"Sure, Lenny." Erin smiled at the man and his face lit up. She watched him walk to the elevator and a pang of sympathy hit her. Nature had played a cruel joke on him. Deeply pitted skin left over from adolescent acne coupled with ears sticking out from his head seemed harsh enough. But his mouth didn't quite fit his face. He held his lips slightly parted so often she wondered if he could close them.

"The guy gives me the creeps," Carol said.

"Says the Christian, Bible-toting woman in the room," Erin chastised.

"I'm polite when he's around. I don't speak negatively about him to anyone—"

Erin raised an eyebrow.

"Except to you. And you don't count because you're my best friend. I tell you everything."

Erin shook her head and gave an exasperated sigh.

"Besides," Carol said. "I don't remember reading anything in the Bible about 'Thou shalt not recognize creeps.'"

"I'm sure there's a passage in there somewhere."

"Tell you what, you find me the passage and I will not only repent, I'll bake the man cookies every week for a month."

"You're just trying to get me to read more of my Bible. I recognize your underhanded ways."

"Is it working?" Carol smiled widely. "Trust me, Erin. The more you read, the more you'll want to read. God will speak to your heart and you'll delve in there all on your own."

Erin mentally pictured the leather-bound Bible that Carol had given her two weeks ago. She'd been reading it every night before bed. She knew what her friend said was true. The words moved her, inspired her, and she found herself getting up a half hour early each morning to read more.

"Why do you dislike Lenny?" Erin asked.

"I don't dislike him. I feel sorry for the guy. I've even put him on my prayer list."

Erin knew her expression revealed her skepticism.

"I have," Carol insisted. "But he's creepy."

"He's probably lonely. It wouldn't kill you to be friendlier to him."

"Okay. You're right. I'll work on it." Carol leaned on the arm of Erin's chair. "Speaking of being friendly, you should be friendlier to Detective Marino. Ever since the Easter parade, the nurses have placed Tony at the top of their eligible bachelor list."

Carol looked Erin straight in the eye. "Anyway, you have to admit he's got the 'it' factor. Maybe it's those brown eyes. Or that drop-dead-gorgeous smile. Or his soft, sensitive side when he leads a parade for kids or accompanies other kids on buses."

Erin laughed and threw her hands in mock surrender. "Okay, enough already. I get the point."

"All I'm saying is if you don't want him, then you better step out of the way before you get trampled by the ladies in line behind you." Carol's eyes softened. "The man is kind to your son…handsome…gets along well with your aunt…handsome…makes you laugh." She placed her index finger to her lip. "Oh, yeah, did I say he's handsome?"

"He's a cop."

"He's a man."

"Yeah, that, too. Strike two." Erin took a swig from her water bottle.

Carol scooted her chair closer. "He's a good man. And we

both know from experience the good ones don't come along very often."

"Isn't that the truth? I haven't met one of those 'good men' yet. I'm beginning to think they belong in the same category as glass slippers," Erin said. "Even if I wanted to take a chance—and I don't—to see if he really is a good guy, I can't. He's a cop."

"Cop is what he does, not who he is."

"We both know that's not true. They don't turn off at five o'clock. They live and breathe their jobs 24/7."

She reached out and cupped one of Erin's hands. "You know I wouldn't suggest something I thought would hurt you. You're my BFF, remember?"

Erin smiled at the memories of the BFF, or Best Friends Forever Club, they had formed in middle school. She squeezed her friend's hand in acknowledgment but remained silent.

"I think you're wrong for not giving this guy a chance," Carol said. "He's the real deal. Single. Hardworking. Kind."

"Yeah, a real Boy Scout," Erin said.

Carol threw up her hands. "What am I going to do with you? This is the kind of man most women pray for. When the Lord blesses you by plunking him smack dab in your path, you don't chase him away."

Erin blinked hard to hold back tears. "I can't. I want to but…I just can't."

After several minutes, Carol said, "Sometimes that baggage you carry around gets pretty heavy, doesn't it?"

"Baggage? It wasn't me who broke my marriage vows and cheated with every cute skirt in town. I'm not the one who deserted my son when he was born less than perfect. And it won't be me who lets another man hurt me again—or my son. I just can't take the chance." Erin ducked her head.

Silence stretched between them.

"Well, if you can't, you can't. Come on." Carol jumped up and pulled Erin from her seat. "No ambulance sirens. The board's cleared. Ride up to the fourth floor with me. Sue Branson's babysitting Amy and they stopped to see the clown. Maybe we'll meet Mr. Right in the elevator. Who knows?"

"Wait a minute." Erin followed Carol onto the elevator. "I thought you said Mr. Cop was my Mr. Right."

"He is," Carol said. The elevator doors slid shut. "Just not Mr. Right Now."

"Since when does the hospital pay for entertainment for the pediatric floor?" she asked as they exited the elevator and elbowed their way through the crowd.

"Since they can get two for the price of one," Carol said. "That's Jim Peters. Sanitation engineer by day. Clown on the side. He loves the kids. He used to come and entertain them after work. The parents and kids loved him so much that Dottie, in Personnel, told me they decided to throw him a couple of extra bucks to do it officially once a month."

A white-faced clown with orange hair, a big nose, a red outlined mouth and a single black tear painted beneath his left eye scooted among the children. He pulled coins from behind their ears. He made tiny action figures mysteriously appear in the pockets of their pajamas.

The clown selected one child, sitting in a wheelchair, and crouched beside him. Pointing to the tear on his cheek, the clown pretended to be sad, bent down closer still, and squirted water at the boy from a flower on his lapel. The boy hit the clown with his balloon. Both child and clown laughed and the clown fell back on the floor. Within moments all the children jumped on the clown, hitting him with their balloons, laughing and rolling over his flattened body.

Erin joined in the laughter. "He *is* great with the kids."

"I know. Amy and I found out about him accidentally. You know how hard it is to get a doctor on weekends. A couple of months ago, Amy had an ear infection. Robert Stone promised he'd take a look after his rounds if I brought her here. We discovered the clown while we were waiting."

"That sounds like something Robert might do."

Carol raised an eyebrow. "I thought it was over between the two of you." She tilted her head. "It is, isn't it?"

"Of course, it's been over for ages."

"That's what I thought you told me. Why did you dump him, anyway?" Carol grinned. "He's not a cop."

Erin shook her head from side to side in mock exasperation at her friend's teasing. "No, he's not a cop. Truthfully, he's really a nice guy."

"I'm beginning to think nice guys don't stand a chance with you, O'Malley."

Erin ignored her.

"So? What did the nice guy do to get dumped?"

Erin shrugged. "I was looking for light and casual. He wasn't. So, I broke it off. When I realized how much I hurt him, I decided to stop dating period. I'm not interested in a relationship with any man. I only dated him to get out and have a little fun with someone I liked and respected. It hadn't dawned on me that it had the potential to turn into something deeper for the other person. I hated that I hurt him. I won't do that again to somebody else."

"Mama."

Carol scooped three-year-old Amy up into her arms and hugged her tight.

Sue Branson followed closely on Amy's heels, whispered a few words in Carol's ear and stepped away.

"Don't know what I'd do without Sue," Carol said. "She babysat Amy for the last three Friday nights for me."

Erin glanced at her friend. "Are you dating again? Why didn't you tell me? I'd watch Amy for you. Who's the lucky guy?"

Carol's face flushed. Before she could reply, a male voice interrupted.

"I thought I saw the three of you over here."

"Hello, Robert." Erin smiled at the six-foot-tall man and watched in amusement as Amy reached out her arms to him. He lifted the child, held her in the crook of his arm and didn't offer a word of protest as she tousled his hair with her hands, laughed and did it again, entertaining herself as if she had invented the game.

"Good to see you, Erin. How have you been?" he asked.

"Just fine, Robert, and you?"

"Good." His eyes no longer held the traces of hurt and anger she had seen after their breakup. With a sense of relief, she realized something else, a sparkle, a genuine happiness seemed to reside there now.

"We're watching the clown show," Carol said. "Or, at least, we were."

The show was over and the clown gone.

Erin glanced at her watch. "No wonder. Look at the time. I have to get back downstairs. It's almost time for shift report. I want to get home before Tess puts Jack to bed."

"I'll be down in a minute," Carol said. "I have to wait for Sue to come back from the restroom."

Erin nodded and slipped away from the group. The elevator was packed to capacity and a second group waited to board. Not wanting to wait, Erin slipped into the stairwell and took the steps two at a time. She had just cleared the second landing when she heard the heavy metal door slam behind her. She smiled. She wasn't the only one too impatient to wait.

Erin exited on the ground floor. A quick glance at her watch made her increase her pace. Her fifteen-minute break had quickly stretched into twenty minutes. Erin needed to hustle and get back to the ER.

The hospital was in the process of building a new facility out near the interstate. The grand opening was set for this summer, but some offices had already been moved and a couple wings of this building already closed. Erin rushed past a door leading to one of the empty wings and then turned around and went back. This wing cut right across the middle of the ground floor. If she took this shortcut, it could save her valuable time she would otherwise spend racing like a rat in a maze through the other corridors. She'd end up in the same place anyway, but this route would get her there in half the time.

Erin warred with herself. She was the kind of person who followed the rules. She didn't claim to be sick when she wasn't. She didn't cheat on her taxes. She stopped at red lights. She did her best to live a good, clean, socially obedient life.

Except for her love of speed. Erin could almost feel an accelerator pedal beneath her foot and grinned.

Ignoring the Caution—Do Not Enter sign, she glanced both ways to make sure she wouldn't be observed breaking the rules and slipped inside. It took her eyes a second to adjust. Instead of the bright fluorescent bulbs throughout the hospital, this area was lit by single bulbs placed strategically along the way. Erin began walking down the dimly lit corridor.

Furniture, file cabinets and medical equipment waiting for transfer to the new facility loomed on all sides of a small walkway and cast monstrous shadows on the floor. The silence made Erin uneasy. Maybe this hadn't been such a good idea. She increased her pace. A rustling sound behind her made Erin pause. Was someone else in this deserted part of the hospital? She stood still and listened.

Nothing.

She continued moving toward the exit.

Bang. The sound of metal hitting the concrete floor echoed through the room. Erin's heart slammed against her chest. Someone was in here with her.

"Hello. Is anybody there?"

Silence.

Why didn't they show themselves? Her breathing quickened and her pulse raced.

Rooted to the spot, she stared into the darkness. She thought she saw a furtive movement in the shadows.

"Hello?"

Ice-cold fingers of fear crept up her spine. Erin wasn't stupid enough to stand around in the darkness waiting for answers that didn't come. She sprinted toward the exit and burst through the door. Never before had she been so happy to see the ebb and flow of people moving through the corridor.

What was the matter with her? Since when was she afraid of the dark? That'll teach her to break the rules. She collapsed against the wall, leaned her head back and tried to catch her breath.

"Miss Erin? Are you okay?"

Erin glanced up. Lenny stood beside her, holding blood specimen tubes housed in plastic bags in both hands.

Erin's chest heaved from the exertion of the last few minutes but she managed to smile.

"I'm fine, Lenny." She pushed off the wall, grateful to see the entrance to the ER straight ahead. "Just getting a little exercise on my break." She nodded and hurried past him.

The rest of her shift passed without incident. After report she waved at Carol and said goodbye to her peers. Erin hurried to the lobby. Her nerves were still on edge and she'd be glad when she was home. She rummaged around the bottom of her purse for her keys and stepped outside. Pausing for a moment in the entranceway, she glanced up.

God, it's so beautiful tonight. Look at those stars. I'm constantly in awe of Your breathtaking creations.

The breeze ruffled her hair. She shoved her hands into her jacket pocket but couldn't find her scarf. She fumbled in her purse, admonishing herself for the hundredth time for owning a purse without separate compartments, and came up empty. Where is it? She chewed her bottom lip. Think. When was the last time you had your scarf?

She shuffled the purse contents. Cell phone. Wallet. Lipstick. Tissues. Paperback.

This color looks good on you, brings out the color of your eyes.

Tony. The silk scarf slipping ever so slowly through his fingers. She stared into her purse. The scarf was gone.

Lost in thought, she walked to her car and almost missed the item tucked beneath her windshield wiper. Erin pulled out the dead, withered rose and opened the small white note wrapped around the stem. She held it under the lamp light and read it. Then, read it again. Her fingers trembled and the note slipped to the ground.

FOUR

Sergeant Greene stood in the front of the room. "Okay, men. What do we have?"

"The autopsy report is back on Cynthia Mayors," Tony said. "Same findings as Anne Morton and Leigh Porter with one difference. She fought back hard enough to provide DNA material for testing."

"Yeah, if we come up with someone to test," Spence grumbled.

"Official cause of death," Tony continued, "in all three cases was exsanguination."

Brad Winters spoke up. "Let me get this straight. He did what he wanted with these women and then what? Did he just pull up a chair and watch them bleed to death? I don't get it."

"Let's hope none of us ever understand that kind of rage," Tony said.

"Where are we with suspects?" Sarge asked.

Spence cleared his throat. "None, Sarge. Zip. Nada."

"Spence and I are going to take another run at the convenience store where Anne Morton worked," Winters said. "Most of us have the habit of frequenting the store closest to our home. You know, the wife calls and you run in to get milk or bread on the way home. Maybe this guy was a regular customer. One night he goes in there and she says or does something that sets him off. Something made her a victim."

"Yeah, Sarge. And if he does live in the area, then the other clerks might recognize him as a regular. We're hoping now that some time has passed and they've gotten over the initial shock of the murder they might remember something."

"All we got out of the manager last time was that Morton was dependable," Winters said. "Never missed a day of work. Even brought her kid to work with her once when her baby-sitter was a no-show."

"Husband? Family? Friends?" Sarge asked.

"None we could find," Spence replied. "The lady went to work and went home to her kid. Period." He leaned back in his chair and sighed audibly.

"Three women. Three different lifestyles with no visible connection," Tony said. "One worked as an assistant manager at a convenience store. One worked as an administrative assistant for a local contracting company. Our third victim was a nurse. Two white, one black. One single, one married and one going through a divorce. Three different neighborhoods, three different economic situations. The only obvious connection is that all three victims have children. Lord help us if that is the only criterion this nutcase uses. Imagine trying to protect all the moms in this world."

Sergeant Greene clamped his teeth down hard on a yellow pencil. After a moment of contemplation, he barked, "Are you suggesting these are random killings? That there's no connection between these victims?" He shook his head. "Don't buy it. There's got to be a common link. Something ties these women together. You're missing it, fellows. Dig deeper."

"That's why we're going back to the convenience store," Winters said. "Maybe we can jog somebody's memory.

Maybe a customer who hung around too much. Or Morton complained to a coworker about a rude comment. Something."

"I might have something," Tony said. "Leigh Porter's pastor called. Something's been nagging at him. He doesn't think it's important, but obviously, whatever it is, he wants to get it off his chest. I made an appointment rather than have him tell me over the phone so I'd have the opportunity to probe a little. Maybe it'll lead somewhere."

"Good. See what you can turn up." The sergeant gathered the papers in front of him and stood. "Let's not waste time. We've got a serial killer to catch."

Tony slid out of his car, arched his back and removed his jacket. He reached into the backseat, withdrew a small bag and hung his jacket on the inside hook above the side window. Before walking up to Erin's front door, he stretched again. It had been a grueling day.

The interview with the pastor at Porter's church had provided a potential lead. The pastor told him about a conversation he had had with Leigh the Sunday before her death. He noted she didn't look quite as perky as usual. She told him she hadn't been sleeping well. She'd been getting anonymous phone calls, mostly at night. When he expressed concern and encouraged her to report the calls to the police, she laughed. With four kids of her own, two of them starting those dreaded teen years, she figured it was just kids playing a prank and they'd tire of the game soon enough. She hadn't thought it important, so Pastor Jones forgot about it. But lately, it'd been niggling at his conscience. What if it wasn't a kid's prank? What if it had something to do with her murder? That's when he thought maybe he'd better call. Tony ordered Porter's phone records pulled.

Then, he'd taken another shot at Leigh Porter's neighbors. House after house, he heard the same story. What a good woman she was. Friendly, outgoing, helpful. Active in her church. Adored her kids. Managed to keep all four of them on the straight and narrow, which wasn't an easy task considering her no-good husband. The man liked to frequent the local bars and came home staggering—when he did come home. He was a nasty drunk. Had a mean temper. Slammed her around a couple of times. She drew the line the day one of their teenage sons tried to protect her and ended up with a broken arm for his trouble. Porter filed for divorce the next day. Right after she had him arrested.

Unfortunately, that gave his number one suspect an ironclad alibi. When Leigh Porter disappeared and was murdered, her husband was in jail.

The closer Tony got to Erin's front door, the more relaxed he felt, almost like he was coming home. The feeling surprised him and his guard went up. He refused to have any feelings about this woman. Period. He rang the bell, peered through the side glass panels and grinned when he saw Tess approach.

She opened the door and gestured him inside. "Detective Marino, what brings you here?"

Tony stepped into the foyer. The long forgotten scent of home cooking caused his stomach to rumble and reminded him that he hadn't eaten. "I'm a detective, ma'am. I followed the world's most delectable aroma all the way from the station and, lo and behold, it led me right here."

Tess chuckled and led him into the kitchen. "Sit. You look like you've had a long day, lad." Once he did, she placed a cup of her Irish coffee in front of him.

He made a show of inhaling deeply before he took a sip. "Perfection."

A satisfied smile danced across Tess's lips. "Surely, you'll be staying for some of my ham and cabbage."

"I appreciate the offer, but I just stopped by for a minute."

"Nonsense. Don't go insultin' me. There's plenty of food. I'll just be settin' another plate at the table."

"Who was at the door?"

Erin stood in the doorway and Tony couldn't suppress his response. She was a beautiful woman. And Christian or not, he was still human—and male. Wisps of wet auburn hair curled in tiny circles, framing her face. An undulating river of dark red fell over her shoulders and covered her chest. Her skin glistened. She looked like she'd just stepped out of a steam bath. Her green eyes widened when she met his gaze but the look of surprise quickly faded when Jack plowed into the back of her heels with his walker.

"Ouch, Jack, watch what you're doing." Erin steadied the walker, allowed the child to pass her and then followed him into the room.

"Detective Marino," Jack yelled. "When did you get here?"

"Just a minute ago, champ." He directed his words to Jack, but his eyes never left Erin. He came to see the boy. But he couldn't deny a strong pull to Jack's mother, a tension that pulsated through his veins every time she entered a room. One temptation he was determined to ignore.

"Tony's joining us for dinner," Tess said. "Set him a place at the table while I tend to the food."

Erin glanced his way. He shrugged and nodded his head toward Tess, indicating he was innocent.

Once seated, Erin bowed her head to say grace before the meal. Dinner conversation flowed easily. Jack chattered nonstop about the field trip. And everyone laughed when he stage-whispered in Tony's ear, loud enough for everyone to hear, that he wouldn't mind if Tony wanted to play his dad again sometime.

Erin joined the conversation, but she also seemed to enjoy sitting back and observing the interaction between Tess, Jack and himself. For the second time in as many weeks, Tony realized how much he enjoyed the feeling of being a part of this family and warning signs flashed through his mind. He had to get out of here. He pushed back his plate, patted his stomach and said, "Ms. O'Malley that was delicious."

"Tess, remember? Thank you, lad." Tess picked up his empty plate and carried it to the sink.

Erin leaned over and whispered, "The way to her heart is through her cooking. You'll be gaining twenty pounds before you know it if you're not careful."

Tony chuckled. "Thanks for the warning."

"Are you taking us to Disney World again?" Jack asked.

"Sorry, champ. Not this time." He lifted a bag from the floor by his chair. "But I did stop by for a reason. Recognize this?"

Jack excitedly snatched the bag and looked inside. "My Mickey Mouse coloring book and my Lego kit. I've been looking all over for them."

Tony answered Erin's unspoken question. "He left them on the backseat of my car. I've been tied up on a case and haven't had a chance to return them."

"You didn't happen to see my green scarf did you?"

"The one that matches your eyes?" He smiled at the instant blush of color that tinged her cheeks. "Don't tell me you lost it." He pretended to be horrified.

Before she could reply, Jack interrupted. "Can I open my Legos, Mom? Please?"

Erin laughed. "Don't give me that sad-eyed puppy dog

look of yours. You're going to turn into a manipulating little scamp if I'm not careful." Mussing his hair, she said, "Play in the living room and make sure you pick up every piece before you get ready for bed."

"I'll supervise the lad." Tess removed the apron from her ample girth. "You sit and visit with your company."

"Alone, at last." Tony grinned and wiggled his eyebrows up and down.

When Erin laughed, he realized just how much he had missed the sweet, tinkling sound. After the field trip, he'd been tied up on the case, and days passed without a word between them. She probably thought he'd been following her request to move on. He should. Part of him wanted to. But one look into her sparkling green eyes and he knew it wasn't something he was ready to do.

"I'm surprised to see you," she said.

"Why? Because you kicked my male ego to the curb?" He smiled and leaned toward her. "I know most men would have probably tucked their tail between their legs and headed for higher ground when you gave them the boot." He captured an auburn strand of her hair and curled it around his finger. "But I'm not most men."

She lowered her eyes and seemed to struggle to find her voice.

"Besides, I know you didn't mean to kick me to the curb. Did you, darling?" he teased.

Erin locked her eyes with his and looked at him with such intensity it stole his breath. There was something happening between them. Something neither one of them seemed to want and neither one could leave alone.

He cleared his throat and subtly straightened back in his own chair where he belonged. Trying to keep his voice businesslike, he said, "Seriously, Erin. We need to talk. A woman filed a complaint at the station, today. She's been receiving upsetting telephone calls."

Erin blinked hard. "It wasn't me. I filed my report a week ago."

"I know," he assured her. "But I found out today that one of our murder victims also got harassing calls."

Erin's eyes widened. "You think…?"

"It's too soon for me to think anything, right now. But it'd be foolish to ignore the coincidence. I wanted to see if you're still being harassed."

"No."

He sensed she wasn't being a hundred percent truthful.

She sipped her coffee, holding the cup with both hands, but it didn't hide her trembling.

"Erin?" His fingers cupped her chin. "You can trust me. You can come to me if you have a problem, any problem."

Erin shivered and a small groan escaped her lips.

He sat quietly. He could wait. He was an expert in interrogation. He'd sit here and wait all night if that's what it took.

"The calls kept coming." Her voice softened to a little more than a whisper. "Even after I let the answering machine screen the numbers I didn't recognize. So I changed to a private number and they stopped."

"Okay." Tony's eyes never left her face. "So why do I feel there's more you're not telling me?"

Obviously, this was difficult for her. He knew Erin was a very private person, kept tight rein on her feelings, maintained an outward appearance of always being in complete control. But now she squirmed beneath his scrutiny. Her mouth twisted into a grim line. Tony continued to sit quietly, not rushing her, letting her tell things in her own time.

"Two nights ago, I found a dead rose under my windshield wiper when I left work. There was a note attached."

"Did you keep the note?"

"No." She stood and moved about the kitchen, idly straightening canisters, fidgeting with salt and pepper shakers, wiping counters. "I wasn't thinking clearly, I guess. I just wanted to forget about it." She threw him a warning glance over her shoulder. "I still do."

"Did you report it?"

"Yes, I drove straight to the Ormond Beach police station before I went home."

"Why didn't you call the sheriff's department?"

"Because I already filed a report about the phone calls with the Ormond police. I figured they were the ones I should tell about the dead rose and note, too. But it was just a waste of time. They typed a report and added it to my file. That's about it."

"Why didn't you call me?"

She blushed, ducked her head and shrugged.

Tony crossed the room and gently turned her to face him. "Tell me about the note."

"What's to tell? Someone likes getting their kicks trying to scare people. I probably should have looked around. I'm sure there were similar notes on dozens of cars, like the flyers tucked beneath your windshield wipers at the mall." She looked at him, her eyes wary, frightened, begging him to assure her it was nothing.

"Humor me. What did it say?"

In an empty tone of voice, almost resigned, she said, "Death knows this rose to be as black as your heart is to thee."

"Death? That's what he calls himself?"

She nodded.

Tony noted her uneasiness, the trembling of her hands, the quiver of her lips.

He pulled her into his embrace, keeping his voice tender, his touch comforting. "It's okay. I'm not going to let anyone hurt you." He surprised both of them by brushing his lips across the top of her head. Immediately he loosened his hold and stepped back.

"I want you to make a formal complaint with the sheriff's office, too."

Erin shook her head. "I've already filed a report. Why do I need to file another one?"

"Sometimes communication fails between the local police departments and the sheriff's department. Prank calls and dead roses could easily be in a category not considered important enough to pass along," he said. "But I want you to report the rose and the telephone calls to the sheriff's department. This could be more serious than you think." He knew the expression on his face was as adamant as he felt.

"You're making a big ado about this," she said. "Truthfully, you're starting to scare me."

"Good. Be scared. I want you to take every precaution. Three women have been brutally murdered. Right here in our own backyard. We don't have a motive. We don't have a suspect. Unfortunately, we don't have much of anything right now. But we do know that at least one of them received harassing telephone calls right before she died. So I want you to be careful. Stay alert. Don't put yourself in any vulnerable situations."

"I got a few prank calls and somebody thought it would be funny to put a dead rose on my car. Stop trying to make me feel like I'm the next victim in a slasher movie." The blood drained out of her face, she couldn't seem to keep her hands busy enough, and he knew she was more afraid than she'd admit.

Good going, Marino. Scare her half to death, why don't you? Some comfort you are.

He studied her quietly. "Look, I'm probably coming on a little too strong."

"Ya think?"

He shrugged. "It's an occupational hazard. Cops tend to see the worst side of a situation."

"Exactly." Her eyes flashed. "I know all about your occupational hazards."

He paused, choosing his words carefully, trying to think of a way to ensure her safety without scaring her more or making her pull away from him altogether. "Maybe you're right. Maybe it's a teenager with too much time on his hands. It's probably not connected to this case at all."

Her eyes held the first glimmer of hope.

"But I still want you to file a report."

Erin sighed loudly.

"And I don't want you to think that what I'm about to say is my way of asking you for a date. I know better than to try that."

A tentative smile crossed her lips.

"But I would like to stop by now and then. Make sure the three of you are safe. Just for my own peace of mind. This would be official business only, of course."

Peace of mind? Around Erin? That's an oxymoron. There's never peace of mind around Erin. There's a ferocious need to protect her. Defend her. Coupled, of course, with a healthy personal interest that just keeps rearing its persistent head no matter how much I don't want it to. Protect and defend. That's my job. Male interest. That's an area I just won't allow myself to act upon.

"What do you say?" He smiled widely and winked.

"Well, if it's official business, Detective, how can I say 'no'?"

FIVE

Two weeks later

Erin ducked her head into the living room to check on Jack and Amy. Satisfied that both children were engrossed in a video, she returned to the kitchen and plopped on a stool.

"Kids okay?" Carol glanced up from the cookbook she'd been perusing.

"Yep. I stood in the doorway for five minutes and they didn't move a muscle. I can't understand how they can be mesmerized by a movie they've seen at least a dozen times."

Carol laughed. "Count your blessings."

"Can you believe it's been two weeks since Easter? Time's been going by in a flash and there never seems to be enough of it."

"I guess a certain detective with a permanent place setting at your dinner table could tend to make time fly, huh?"

Erin rolled her eyes. "Let me guess. Tess has been running at the mouth again."

"I never disclose my sources. But you can't deny it. I've driven by and seen his car once or twice myself. Looks like you took my advice and decided to give the guy a chance."

"I am not dating Detective Marino."

Carol raised an eyebrow.

"I'm not. He's a professional mooch. He praises Tess's cooking. He knows it automatically gets him an invitation for dinner."

"Wow, a winker and a freeloader. There's no end to this man's vices."

Erin shot her a look.

"And after dinner?"

Erin shrugged nonchalantly. "He stays for a while. Sometimes he plays video games with Jack, or he dries the dishes while Tess bends his ear." Erin lowered her eyes and stirred her coffee. "A few times we've sat on the porch and talked. But we are definitely not dating."

"Semantics, girl. Who do you think you're fooling? You know you like him. Why don't you admit it?"

"Of course, I like him. My stomach plunges to the floor every time I get within ten feet of him."

"So? When does the real dating begin? Or is he just eye candy for you?"

Erin laughed and tossed a rumpled up napkin at her friend. "We have an unspoken agreement. He doesn't ask me for a date and I don't interfere with him getting home-cooked meals on a regular basis."

Carol tilted her head to the side and studied Erin. "And you haven't claimed this wonderful man as your own because? Let me guess. You're still in your no-man-in-my-life-ever-again phase. And let's not forget he's a cop, too." Carol's expression darkened. "I can't believe you're so stubborn you're blowing a potentially perfect relationship over his job. I don't get it."

"It isn't his job…not completely."

"Wait. Before you say another word about him being a cop, answer one question. What do you think of him as a man?"

"He's the nicest guy I've ever met. There's a quiet strength and dependability about him." Erin, lost in thought, stared into space. "He's so good with Jack. He's wrapped Tess around his little finger. She thinks the man can do no wrong."

"Have you had a chance to talk with him about his religious beliefs?"

"No. But I know he's a Christian. He's passed all of Tess's tests and has graduated to saying grace at the table now whenever he's over."

"He's a Christian. He's good with both Jack and Tess. He's a nice guy. I get that. But you haven't answered my question. What do *you* think of the man?" Carol stopped looking at the pictures in the cookbook and stared intently at her friend.

Erin met her gaze. "I've never been so drawn to a man before in my life." Her voice trembled. "If I let my guard down…"

Carol waited for her to continue.

"I could fall in love with a man like this," Erin whispered. "The forever-kind-of-love where there are no shields and I open my heart. The thought scares me to death."

Carol squeezed her hand. "Honey, why are you tormenting yourself like this?"

"Because I don't want to follow in my mother's footsteps."

"You're nothing like your mother."

"I know. And I'm determined to keep it that way. I remember my parents' arguments. Smashed dishes. Thrown glasses." Erin absently rubbed her wrist, remembering other casualties of those past disputes.

"Your mother was a mean drunk. Why do you think I hated coming over to your house?"

"My mother was a *lonely* woman who hated being married

to a cop in a generation when divorce was a dirty word and people lived out their lives in misery. Dad never seemed to be around when she needed him. Every school recital, holiday, most dinners, my mother was alone. Even when he was home, he wasn't. He'd bury himself in the study and work."

"Erin, your mother was an active alcoholic who abused her husband, her child and herself. You can't blame your dad's job for that or your dad."

"Can't I?" Erin knew her voice revealed her pain, but she couldn't help it.

Carol's eyes misted. "Honey, you're carrying around a whole lot of anger and bitterness. It's time to give that burden to the Lord. He'll help you if you let Him. You need to learn to forgive."

Erin sighed. "Easier said than done…this forgiveness thing is the toughest part for me."

"I know," Carol said. "But God wants us to forgive. He asks us to love one another and leave the judging part to Him." She patted Erin's hand. "Trust me. My own experience has taught me you'll feel a thousand percent better when you let all that ugly, burdensome stuff go and just turn it over to the Lord."

"I wish I could. I remember when I was seven we were evacuated for an impending hurricane. My mother pleaded with Dad not to leave us. She was terrified. We both were. But he was a cop. It was his job to protect the public, not his family. So, he left.

"Mom and I drove in bumper-to-bumper traffic for hours. The hotels were full everywhere we went until we found a room in this dark, smelly hole-in-the-wall. Mom started drinking heavier than usual. I was scared and I kept asking for Daddy. She got so mad at me," Erin whispered. "That was my first broken bone. I told the doctor I fell off the bed."

"Erin, I'm so sorry." Carol put an arm around her friend's shoulders. "I can't believe you never told me. I used to think you were just a giant klutz with all your bumps and bruises and casts. Why didn't you tell me?"

Erin saw tears in her friend's eyes and hugged her. "What could you have done? What could anybody have done? I thought it was my fault. And I was afraid if I told it would make my mother madder." Erin carried her empty cup to the sink.

"Did your father know?" Carol asked.

"I never told him. He never asked. He accepted Mom's explanations without question." Memories taunted her. "Except once." Erin turned toward Carol. "I had my wrist in a cast, again. He stood in the doorway with an odd expression on his face. Like he was bracing himself for something horrible. He asked me if I really did trip over my skates."

"What did you tell him?" Carol asked.

"I was nine and scared of my mother's anger. What do you think I told him?" She forced herself to smile. "Anyway, it's all past history. A closed door I don't often open."

"You're an adult now and a nurse to boot. You can't really believe your dad's job caused your mother's drinking, do you?"

Erin fought tears. "I know it didn't help. I was seventeen when drunk driving claimed her life." Erin poured herself a glass of water and took a sip. "It was bound to happen sooner or later. But I often wondered if he had been home that day. Maybe if he had been there…"

Carol's gaze locked with hers. "Maybe he couldn't be. Maybe he tried for years and the booze pushed him away until he gave up."

Erin's temper warmed her cheeks, but she didn't reply.

Carol's voice softened. "If I remember correctly, your dad was there when you needed him. After Jack's dad took off, what did you do? You crawled home to Papa. And what did he do? He welcomed you back. That's what good fathers do, Erin. Just like God. God opens His arms and welcomes us back. He showers us with His love and healing."

Erin wiped a tear from her cheek, but remained silent.

"Your dad, even though he was a cop, was there for you…and for Jack…at one of the lowest times of your life. What if his job had nothing to do with your mom's problems? So your dad wasn't perfect. Who is? He coped with a terrible situation the only way he knew how, even if it wasn't the best way."

"I don't deal with maybes or what-ifs anymore," Erin said. "I deal with facts. Fact—a cop's job puts a tremendous strain on families. Fact—cops have a high divorce rate. Fact—marriage is hard enough without starting out with one strike against you. I tried it once with Jack's father. We both know how that turned out. So, I don't date cops. I don't trust men. And I never will again."

An uncomfortable silence filled the room with a heaviness that couldn't be seen or touched.

"I'll pray for you, Erin. That you find your way to forgiveness. Only then will you ever know peace."

Erin didn't respond.

After a moment, Carol said, "We'll just have Tony quit his job and become your personal eye candy. Now, come over here and tell me what you think of this recipe."

Erin perched on the stool beside her friend and made a pretense of being interested in the picture. After a moment, she sighed deeply. "Personal eye candy. I like that."

They looked at each other and laughed.

"Don't touch my cookie dough," Erin warned.

You'd think the scent of cookie dough and vanilla would

have triggered matronly images in his mind, but Erin could tell from the glint in his eyes that the last thought on Tony's mind was his mother. She felt his gaze trace her features. Suddenly, she felt like a deer caught in the headlights of an oncoming car.

But a hooded look darkened his eyes and she could sense a slight withdrawal. That happened a lot lately. He'd seem on the verge of saying or doing something intimate and then he'd pull back. What was that all about? Did he have secrets of his own? The push-pull of his emotions intrigued her.

Tony scooped a dollop of dough from the bowl on his index finger and held it out. "Want to try?"

"Ewww!" She swatted in the air at his hand. "Are you crazy?"

Tony kept a straight face, but the occasional twist to his lips made her think he was roaring with laughter on the inside. He seemed to love to tease her and didn't stop until he had succeeded in causing a rush of color to her cheeks. Pointedly trying to ignore him, she asked, "Did your mom bake a lot when you were a kid?"

"Mom baked every Christmas," Tony replied, "and let me lick the leftover batter."

Erin glanced at the hand inching her way and snatched the bowl protectively to her chest. "Don't even think about it."

He grinned.

"What's the matter?" Erin asked. "She only bakes for holidays so you're coming over here to harass me? Have her give me a call. I'll gladly share my chocolate chip recipe."

"Mom's on an extended vacation with her new husband."

Erin digested the information. "You haven't mentioned your family before."

Tony shrugged. "Just Mom, me and my older sister. My dad was a cop, killed in the line of duty when I was three. I don't remember much about him. But—" he locked his eyes with hers "—I remember how much I missed having a dad around. I guess that's why I have a soft spot for Jack."

She pictured Tony as a little boy wishing for a dad, just like Jack, and her heart melted. Erin sighed. "I wish I could do more for Jack."

"You're a great mom," Tony said. "I have total respect for single moms. They have to pull double duty even knowing it's an impossible task."

"Is that how you feel about your mom?"

"Absolutely. Love her to pieces and owe her the world."

"And your sister? Are you close?" Erin shocked herself at her boldness, but couldn't seem to stop.

"We're super close…or as close as a person can be to someone who lives thousands of miles away. Janet's husband is a Colorado ski instructor. They have three kids, one girl and two boys."

"Wow, Colorado. That is far. Do you ski?"

Tony laughed. "I can handle the intermediate slopes with my nephews. Those two rascals love to boast that they taught me everything I know."

"You seem to really like kids. Do you mind if I ask why you haven't started a family of your own?"

"Boy, this cookie dough is coming at a steep price," Tony teased.

A warmth rushed into Erin's cheeks. "I'm sorry. I shouldn't be so nosy."

Tony chuckled. "Chill out. I was only teasing. How else are you going to get to know me?" His voice deepened and his eyes darkened. "And that's what we're doing, right? Getting to know one another."

The heat in her cheeks intensified.

"In answer to your question," Tony said, "I haven't started a family of my own for a multitude of reasons. My job for one. Sometimes cops don't come home. I know what that feels like. I never want to chance that happening to one of my own."

Erin nodded her understanding.

"Not to mention that my Christian beliefs require marriage before parenthood. I haven't been actively looking for a candidate for that forever-after role. Any nominations come to mind?" He grinned and winked, melting her heart with those chocolate eyes of his.

"Besides," he said, his tone sobered, "any man can father a child, but it takes something special to be a dad. I never wanted to take the test—and fail." The honesty and intensity in his expression pierced her to the soul.

The front door burst open and they heard Jack lumber down the hall. "I hate this walker," he yelled and slammed his bedroom door behind him.

Erin jumped to her feet, but Tony placed a hand on her forearm.

"Please. Let me. Jack told me he was having problems with some boys at school."

"He told *you?*"

Tony shrugged noncommittally. "It was man-to-man stuff."

"Man-to-man? Are you crazy? That's my five-year-old baby in there and you—" Her body temperature rose to lava-spewing levels.

"Erin, calm down."

"I will not calm down. You have no right to—"

"I know I don't."

His sudden acquiescence took the wind out of the verbal storm she was about to unleash.

"I'm not trying to step between you and your son," Tony

assured her. "I just think, based on my prior conversation with Jack, I might be able to help. Let me try." He waited for his words to have an impact.

Erin knew her emotions were in danger of flaring out of control but she didn't care. How could he talk with Jack about a problem at school and not tell her? And why did Jack go to him in the first place? Does he miss having a dad more than she thought? *What should I do, Lord? I know what I want to do. I want to tell Tony to mind his own business.* She glanced at the man sitting quietly, waiting for her decision. *No, I don't. He grew up without a dad. He understands better than me how Jack feels.*

Erin lowered her gaze and nodded permission.

Tony heard muffled crying behind the door. He rapped lightly and, without waiting for an invitation, entered the room. The boy lay facedown on the bed, his face buried in a pillow.

"Hey, buddy."

"Go away."

Tony pushed the walker to the side and sat on the bed.

"Tough day at school?"

"I don't want to talk about it. Go away."

Tony picked up a box of tissues from the dresser and saw Jack peeking at him from beneath his folded arms. He dumped the tissues in the trash, reached into his back pocket, withdrew a clean, white handkerchief and offered it to Jack. "Here. I think it's time you had your own grown-up handkerchief."

Jack's hand reached out for the folded cloth and a ghost of a smile touched his lips. He sat up, swiped at his nose and stopped crying. "Men use handkerchiefs, not boys."

"That's right." Tony smiled.

The boy's expression darkened as he seemed to be remembering the events of the day but he didn't cry.

"Did your friends dump you again today to play ball?" Tony asked.

Jack shook his head side to side.

"What, then?"

A tiny whisper filled the room. "They went bike riding."

Tony's heart seized at the pain vibrating in Jack's voice. He knew he shouldn't be letting himself get attached to the boy. It was one thing to play a video game or spend a day at a theme park. It was quite another to be offering advice and comfort like he was his real dad.

"I can't play ball. I can't ride bikes." Jack's shoulders sagged. "I hate being different."

"Everybody's different."

Jack looked at Tony, doubt, anger and disappointment all scrunched together on his face.

"It's true," Tony assured him. "Every person on earth is a one-and-only model. No two alike."

"Uh-uh. Twins aren't different."

Tony grinned. "Uh-huh, even twins." He ruffled the boy's hair. "Twins might look alike, but they're different people with their own feelings and their own talents and their own way of doing things. Just because people look alike or even dress alike doesn't make them the same person, does it?"

Jack shook his head.

"Let me ask you a question. Did those boys walk with you to class today?"

Jack nodded.

"Did they sit at the lunch table with you?"

He nodded again.

"See, Jack. They're your friends. Just because you can't do *everything* with them doesn't mean they don't like you."

Tony rested an arm across the boy's shoulders, cradling

him gently against his side. "There is only one you, Jack. Your friends like you just the way you are."

Jack lowered his head. "But I wanted to go bike riding with them."

"I understand, buddy. But sometimes we don't get everything we want." He lifted the boy's chin. "We'll just have to come up with other things you can do together."

"Like what?"

"Like go to a movie or have a sleepover."

"What movie?"

"I don't know. We'll have to look in the paper and see what's playing."

The boy's shoulders sagged again.

"Or I could borrow a police car and take your friends for a ride. I might even run the siren."

Jack's eyes widened. "A real police car! Can we, Tony? Really?"

"Absolutely."

Jack grinned. "Wait until I tell Mom." He grabbed his walker, today's disappointment already forgotten, and headed for the bedroom door.

SIX

Carol weaved through the cafeteria crowd like a drunken sailor on the *Titanic*. Arriving without spillage, she placed the tray on the table and plopped down beside Erin. "People are so inconsiderate."

"Sounds like someone woke up on the grumpy side of the bed today," Erin said.

"Don't start. I'm not irritable."

Erin's eyes widened, but she knew better than to speak.

Carol looked at her friend. "What? Okay, maybe I'm a little grumpy."

Erin laughed and slid her chocolate pudding onto Carol's tray. "Here, you need it more than I do."

Carol grinned. "That bad, huh?"

"How can I help?"

Before she could answer Lenny approached with tray in hand. "Hi, Erin. Mind if I join you?"

"Sorry, Lenny," Carol interjected. "These seats are saved. We're waiting for friends and there won't be room today."

Erin blinked in astonishment at her friend's comments.

Lenny glared at Carol, then turned his attention to Erin. "I guess we'll have to make it another time."

Erin opened her mouth to speak, but Carol spoke first. "Another time would be good."

Lenny's expression darkened. He made a point not to look in Carol's direction. "Bye, Miss Erin." As he turned, he tripped over his own feet and fell on the floor.

Erin jumped up from the table. "Are you okay? I'm so sorry." She squatted beside him and swept her napkin over the spilled food. Mr. Peters, the janitor, rushed over, grasped Lenny's arm and helped the man to his feet. As Lenny shuffled toward the door, Mr. Peters shot a disapproving glare at both Erin and Carol and went back to emptying the cafeteria trash cans.

Erin's cheeks burned with anger and embarrassment. She turned on her friend with a vengeance. "Why did you do that?"

"I'm sorry. I really am." Carol bowed her head. "I can't help it," she mumbled. "The guy gives me the creeps."

Erin fought to keep her voice down. "I didn't think you had a mean bone in your body. You deliberately hurt him. What's going on?"

"I haven't been sleeping well lately." Carol played with her food.

"That's your excuse?" Erin placed her fists on her hips.

"I know. I shouldn't have spoken to him like that." An angry expression twisted her mouth. "Even if part of me feels he deserved it."

"No one deserves to be purposely embarrassed," Erin said. "What's going on with you?" She recognized guilt in Carol's eyes. And there was something more. Fear?

"I've been getting anonymous phone calls," Carol said.

Erin drew in a deep breath. "You never told me about any calls."

"In the beginning, I thought it was just a prank. I let the

answering machine handle the calls. It didn't work. Eventually, I changed my number."

Erin took a hard look at her friend and noticed for the first time the dark circles beneath her eyes. Her jumpiness and irritability started to make sense.

"The calls started again on my unlisted number," Carol said. "They're worse than before. Now…"

"Now?" Erin prodded.

"He whispers. It's almost like a sick game. The harder you try to listen, the lower he speaks."

Erin slid her hand across the table and caught Carol's fingertips with her own.

"It's a creepy whisper," Carol said. "Sends chills down my spine. I hate myself for listening."

"What does he say?"

"He says his name is Death and he is right behind me."

A sharp pain seized Erin's chest. She couldn't catch her breath. Her own calls, the dead rose and the sick poem flashed through her mind. Should she tell Carol? She took one look at the haggard expression on her friend's face and decided not to add to her stress. "What does this have to do with Lenny? Do you think he's making the calls?"

"He has to be. Only a handful of friends have my new number. And none of them would do this."

"But that doesn't make sense. Lenny isn't your friend. How could he get the number?"

"I don't know. Maybe he got it from Personnel. He probably made up a sob story about needing to get in touch with me about a blood specimen or something."

"Listen to yourself. That's crazy."

"It has to be him," Carol insisted. "I bet he gets his kicks scaring women because he can't find one who will give him the time of day."

"That's a pretty big leap. I admit he's a loner and I'll even admit he's a bit odd. But if that's your only reason—"

Carol raked both hands through her hair. "A few weeks ago, Lenny walked into the nurse's station with two cups of coffee. He plopped one of the cups and himself on the edge of my desk. I thanked him but told him I wasn't interested. Instead of getting mad, he just smiled." Carol visibly shuddered. "It was a creepy smile. He looked me straight in the eye and said, 'Maybe you'll have more time for me if I call first.' The anonymous calls started up again right afterwards."

"Have you called the police?" Erin asked.

"You? Recommending the police? Now I know the world is ending." Carol took a bite of her salad. "Yes, I called them."

"When?"

"About two weeks ago for all the good it did me. Seems prank calls aren't a priority."

Erin chewed on her bottom lip. "Let's run it past Tony. He'll know what to do."

Carol's lips curved in an affectionate smile. "Tony, huh? I heard he's a hero with the neighborhood kids. The line was two deep waiting for a turn to ride in a police car."

"Does Tess give you daily updates on all my business?"

"Don't be mad at Tess. We both love you and have your best interest at heart."

Refusing to get caught up in this discussion, Erin changed the subject. "I still think you need to tell Tony about the calls and your suspicions about Lenny."

"I will," Carol assured her. "But tomorrow's Amy's birthday. I'm not going to let anything put a damper on it. She's so excited about having a party, she can hardly sleep."

Both moms chuckled. Conversation turned to children, birthdays and balloons. For the moment, telephone calls, sleepless nights and fear faded away.

"Give me good news, men," Sergeant Greene addressed the morning briefing.

"I wish I could, boss," Winters said. "Cynthia Mayors's husband is back from Iraq. I met with him yesterday. He's taking both kids to his mother's in Idaho. The guy's so grief-stricken he's operating on autopilot. These two ran off to Vegas, eloped, had a weekend honeymoon and then he shipped out. Now he's got no wife. He's gonna be raising two kids he barely knows and one of them is a seven-year-old autistic boy who doesn't understand what happened. Keeps asking for his mother. Life's a poke in the eye sometimes, Sarge." He paused for a moment and genuine empathy showed on his face.

Winters shuffled through the pages of his notepad. "The neighbor, who spray-painted Anne Morton's house with obscenities after she called the cops on him for his loud parties, has an ironclad alibi. We've tried offering a reward on Crime Line for any new information, but nothing yet."

"Ditto for Leigh Porter," Spence added. "No suspects. No leads. No nothing." He saw Sarge eye his cigarette, so he ground it out.

Sarge chewed on a yellow pencil.

"I spoke to Leigh Porter's pastor," Tony said. "He told me she'd been getting harassing phone calls. I pulled the phone records. Most of them were made using a prepaid disposable cell phone. We traced the cell phone order, but the name and address were phony. Others came from pay phones in public places. Nothing helpful."

Following a light knock, a woman entered the room, stopping further conversation. Sarge gestured for her to join him in the front of the room. "I want you to meet Special Agent Jackie Davidson. She's here at my request. She's worked up a profile on this guy."

The front legs of Spence's chair hit the floor with a bang. "Sorry," he said when all eyes turned toward him. "I get overexcited about FBI help."

"Shut up and listen," Sarge said. "You might learn something."

Davidson, nonplussed by Spence's outburst, opened a manila folder and said, "Good morning, gentlemen. I'm sure you know by now that you're dealing with a serial killer."

"Ya think?" Spence ducked the glares tossed his way.

"Most serial killers are motivated by a variety of psychological factors," Davidson said. "Dysfunctional families, abuse in childhood or maybe a humiliation."

"You'd make a great witness for the defense," Spence mumbled. "The pervert couldn't help himself. He killed the women because his mama hit him with a belt or kids in school called him a sissy."

The sergeant's eyes bulged. "Spence, can it or you're outta here."

Spence glared in the sergeant's direction but remained silent.

"What can you tell us, Agent Davidson?" Tony asked, trying to get things back on track before Spence and Sarge came to blows.

"I made a careful analysis of all three cases," Davidson said. "You have a disorganized killer on your hands. Probably in his late thirties, early forties. Socially inadequate. Has few, if any, friends. When you do catch him, you'll hear acquaintances describe him as a loner, eccentric, possibly creepy."

Winters muttered under his breath. "Creepy? Spence, where were you the night of April 10th?"

Spence sneered at his partner but remained silent.

"Why disorganized?" Tony asked. "His crime scenes are clean. He hasn't left any clues."

"Because the location of the body is not your crime scene. Locate his car or his home and you'll find enough evidence to lock him up for life."

"What about the victims? Is this guy just pulling women off the street? No connection between them? No planning for the big event?" Winters asked.

"This is definitely not random. There is a strong connection between these women. The killings are his emotional signature. His choices may not be logical to us, but all these women satisfy the emotional reasons he kills. And it's possible, even probable, he watches them for days, weeks, maybe even months before he strikes. But the crime itself is opportunistic. He may be watching several women in the same time frame. When the urge to strike becomes more than he can handle, he doesn't plan it out. He snatches the one most accessible at the time."

Davidson made eye contact with each man in the room. "Remember, this man is socially inept. These women aren't cooperating. He's doing a blitz attack and overpowering them."

"You don't happen to have his home address?" Spence asked.

Davidson smiled. "Wish I did, Detective. I understand your frustration. And I know you're racing the clock. He will kill again, soon." She poured a glass of water and took a sip before continuing. "This man stalks his victims, watches them, learns their routines, their habits. When he gets the opportunity to strike, he overpowers them, takes them to another location and tortures them for a prolonged period of time. The actual murder scene is a familiar location where he feels safe."

Davidson sipped her water. "Rage is his motivation. He's punishing them.

"Your killer knows these women or, at least, thinks he does," Davidson continued. "They've angered him. Notice that he doesn't use a weapon. He uses his fists."

Tony'd like to get this guy alone in a dark alley and show him what fists feel like. A quick glance around the table showed he wasn't the only one affected by the agent's words.

"How is he choosing his victims?" Tony asked.

"Your suspect believes these women have committed unforgivable sins against society. Let's consider the Green River killer. He killed over ninety women before he was caught, almost all of them prostitutes. It's the same idea. In his mind, these women need to be punished for something each one of them did, the same crime."

Winters leaned back in his chair. "These women weren't prostitutes. Just moms trying to live their lives."

"Nonetheless, in the killer's mind there is a strong, logical link between all of them," Davidson insisted. "Remember, the link you're seeking isn't something as obvious as attending the same church or living in the same neighborhood. These women probably never even met. But to him they all committed the same *sin*. Discover the common sin and you'll find your killer."

Sergeant Greene shook hands with Davidson and escorted her to the door. When he returned, he said, "This investigation needs to focus on finding the common thread. Where did their paths cross? How did they meet this lowlife? Leigh Porter is the only black woman. Is that significant or coincidental? Winters, I want you to—"

Winters cleared his throat. "Sarge, we've been working around the clock for weeks and haven't turned up a thing. There's no link."

A pregnant pause hung in the air.

Sarge stared hard at each of them. "You're right, Winters. We've been working hard. And we don't have anything to show for it." He rubbed his hand across his jaw. "Look, I understand. You're tired. Frustrated. I get it. But you heard Davidson. This guy is socially inept. He doesn't have family or close friends. Loneliness might be his trigger and sends him on the prowl. So we're going to work a little harder and a little longer to save the next poor woman's life."

Erin's hand trembled. She lowered the receiver into the cradle.

"It's him, again, isn't it?"

Erin, startled at the sound of her aunt's voice, spun around and forced a smile on her face. "I don't know what you're talking about."

"And I don't know when you started to think it was all right to lie to me."

She sighed. "Sorry. I didn't want you to worry."

"What I want to know is what you're going to do about the calls?"

Glancing over her shoulder, Erin shushed her aunt. "I don't want Jack to hear us."

"Jack is sound asleep." Tess poured two cups of coffee and placed one in front of Erin. "No more stalling. The way I see it, these calls started back up about two days ago. Am I right?"

Erin nodded.

"So much for havin' a private number. Have you told Tony?"

"No. He's been busy with a case. But I did file a complaint with the police."

Tess stared at her. "You don't believe these calls are teen-agers and neither do I."

"No, I don't. Worst of all, I'm not the only one getting them."

Tess's eyes widened. "Who else?"

Erin sipped her coffee and squared her shoulders, preparing to deliver the bad news. "Carol. She changed her number, too. But the calls started again. Mostly at night. Poor thing is getting really stressed from sleep deprivation."

Tess frowned at the news.

"There's more," Erin said. "Carol called me earlier tonight. Someone sent a package to her house with rotten fruit and a nasty note inside." Erin saw fear in her aunt's eyes, but neither one of them acknowledged it. Speaking the words aloud would make the danger real.

"I want you to get on that phone this minute. Call Tony and tell him what's going on," Tess demanded.

"Calm down." Erin patted her aunt's hand. "He's busy right now with an important case."

"He won't be too busy for you."

Erin slid her arm around the older woman's shoulders. "I'll tell him. I promise. Tomorrow night after Amy's birthday dinner."

Concern shone in her aunt's eyes.

"I promise I'll take care of it." Erin crossed the room and took the receiver off the hook. "See. No more calls tonight. Now stop worrying. Tomorrow's a busy day. Carol will be over with Amy. And I invited Mr. Fitzgerald for dinner."

"You did what?" Her aunt's eyes widened and her hand automatically patted her hair. "And you didn't tell me?"

"I'm telling you now." Erin grinned. "Our neighbor's all alone. I thought he might like a good home-cooked meal."

"I'm the one cooking this home-cooked meal. I should have a say-so in who gets to eat it."

Erin bit her lower lip to hide her smile at the look of feigned indignation on her aunt's face. Tess had been talking over the fence with the man for years. The past few months those talks had subtly changed to flirting. She knew Tess was pleased about the invitation. Unable to resist the urge to tease her, Erin said, "You're absolutely right. Should I make an excuse and take back the invitation?"

"You can't go askin' a man to dinner and then turn around and take it back. That wouldn't be neighborly. I just wish I'd known. I need time to prepare."

Erin chuckled as she watched her aunt hurry down the hall, probably already lost in thought about choosing a dress. Romance has no age barriers and Erin loved helping Cupid along. She rinsed the cups and was about to leave the kitchen when the phone caught her attention. She considered putting it back on the hook. What if someone needed to get in touch with her? The hospital? Or Carol? Or Tony? She decided to leave her cell phone on, but this house needed one night of silence. Peace. Sleep. She left it off the hook.

Erin turned off the light and looked out the window over the kitchen sink. *Who are you?* Her eyes scanned the shadows in the yard. *Why are you doing this? What do you want?*

The lightheartedness of a few moments ago vanished. She pictured the violet circles under Carol's eyes and heard the edginess in her voice. She pictured the fear in her aunt's eyes. She thought about the withered black rose left on her windshield and a chill raced up her spine.

I don't know who you are, you creep. But I refuse to let you frighten me. She stared out into the darkness. *Yeah, right.*

SEVEN

Tony shuffled through the folders on his desk, pulling one out. Flipping it open, he stared at the photo inside. Okay, Leigh, tell me how you met this guy? Help me find him.

He was missing something. He could feel it. But he'd gone over the material a hundred times. Still, something nagged at his subconscious. Something he heard. Something someone said. He squeezed his eyes shut and tried to concentrate. What was it?

He stretched in his chair, cupping his hands behind his neck. Every muscle in his body protested from bending over these files for hours and neglecting his daily workout. He needed to get out of here. Stretch his legs. Maybe jog a little. Get the cobwebs out of his mind.

Eyeing the phone, he thought about someone else he'd neglected lately. He knew he shouldn't have accepted Erin's invitation to Amy's birthday dinner. She needed to start spending time with someone she could build a future with, not someone who was married to his job.

His mind conjured up a picture of Erin with another man and an uncomfortable sensation twisted his gut. He reached for the phone and dialed her number before he could change his mind. Saved by a busy signal. He shifted in his chair.

*Okay, buddy. Repeat after me. Erin hates cops. I am a cop.
Erin needs commitment. I am commitment-phobic. Should be
a no-brainer.* So why couldn't he get her out of his mind?

Tony thought about the telephone calls, the dead rose, the
poem and found the whole situation unsettling. At least one
of the victims had received harassing calls and the possibility,
no matter how remote, of Erin being in danger was unaccept-
able. He had to find the killer. He leaned forward and
reopened a file.

Erin lathered herself with lilac body wash. The hot shower
spray's pulsating massage hit the back of her neck, rolled
across her shoulders and flowed down her spine. She could
feel the tension of the day disappear.

She knew she had to tell Tony everything. No more half
truths. No more trying to handle things alone. The Lord
reminded her of the foolishness of pride when she opened her
Bible earlier and read 1 Corinthians 8:2, "If anyone thinks he
knows all the answers, he is just showing his ignorance."

Reality hit her hard. Depending on others made her uncomfortable. She particularly didn't want to have to depend on a
man. Even if the man in question had proven a dozen times
he could be depended upon.

Carol often cautioned her about trying to run her own life.
Encouraged her to turn the reins over to the Lord, pray daily,
listen for His wisdom and direction. Let Him put people in
her path to assist when needed. Tony definitely stood right in
the middle of her path, didn't he?

Erin stepped from the shower, toweled off and slipped into
her pajamas. What was the matter with her? Whenever Tony was
around she became a stereotype of a love-sick teenager, flirty,
silly, giggling. Why couldn't she just be friends with the man?

Her eyes locked with her mirror's reflection and she knew the answer. Because he was the kind of man she had dreamed about her entire life. She pictured him leaning in the kitchen doorway, his hair tousled, his jacket thrown carelessly over his shoulder, with that crooked, come-hither smile on his face.

She thought about how right it felt to see him sitting across the table at dinner. Drying dishes with Tess. Playing video games with Jack. He proved himself over and over to be dependable, capable and self-assured.

And he liked her, too. He didn't want to. She chuckled to herself. Over the past month, she'd seen him war with his feelings. He'd be laughing or talking or just genuinely enjoying himself. Then he'd catch himself. His eyes would darken, like he physically pulled down a curtain, and she could sense a change. A push-pull reaction of wanting to be here with her, with Jack and then not wanting to be. She couldn't be disappointed or angry about it. She happened to be in the same boat. Wanting to let her guard down. Wanting to trust a man again. But she wouldn't survive the pain if she dared to trust Tony and he broke her heart.

Erin just couldn't get past her fear. After her divorce, followed so closely by her father's death, she had devoted herself to Jack, Tess and her job. She'd pretended an outward facade of self-assurance and strength until, one day, it became the truth. She toughened up and took control of her life. A life with no room for love.

Love makes you vulnerable. Suddenly, you're accountable to someone else for everything. Even your own personal space is no longer just your own. Erin felt safe in her private little world and Tony, a man she knew she could never control, threatened that comfort zone.

A small voice inside told her change isn't always bad.

Adding Tony to their lives could enrich it. *Was* enriching it. But if she listened to that voice, she'd be putting everything she held dear at risk and she didn't think she had that kind of courage.

Erin slipped between the sheets and stared sightlessly at the ceiling. *Please help me, Lord. What is Your will for my life? Should I take a chance on Tony? Do I dare dream it could all work out?*

A subtle rustling in the darkness drew her attention to her open bedroom door. Was Jack sneaking out of his room? No. The subtle sound was not made by a five-year-old with a walker. Erin held her breath and strained to listen. There it was again. Someone was in her house.

She grabbed the phone to call 911. The line was dead. She'd left an extension off the hook in the kitchen. Now what? Her cell phone. She grimaced the moment the thought popped into her head. She'd left it charging overnight on the kitchen counter. Her choice was made. She slipped on her robe and searched the room for a weapon. Standing in her closet doorway, she frowned at the shoe in her hand. What damage did she think she could do with a stiletto? She couldn't even walk in the stupid things let alone stop a burglar with one.

Still, it was better than nothing. She'd aim for the eyes. Aim for the eyes? Was she crazy? She'd better not get close enough to see this bad guy's eyes or she'd probably faint. Tucking the shoe into the pocket of her robe, she tiptoed into the hall, her bare feet soundless against the hardwood floor. She paused. Silence. She waited a few minutes more. Nothing.

The tension in her shoulders eased. *I'm letting those phone calls turn me into a basket case.* She started to turn back.

There it was again. The sound came from the direction of the living room. She had to get to the kitchen and phone for help. Erin paused while her eyes adjusted to the darkness. Why had she been so stupid and taken the phone off the hook?

She padded down the hallway, carefully avoiding the darker shadows of furniture and plants in her path. Trying not to reveal her presence, she inched toward the kitchen. Every step seemed to take a lifetime. Every creak of the floorboards froze her in place until she felt safe enough to proceed.

The sounds from the living room intensified as she drew closer.

Ten more feet to the kitchen. Fear squeezed her throat. Her breath came in shallow, short puffs. She entered the kitchen and grabbed a butcher knife from the knife block on the counter. Stupid idea. He can *use it on you.* Still, it gave her a false sense of security and anyone would have had a hard time prying it out of her fingers.

Only a few more steps and she'd be able to reach the phone.

She crept forward. Blood rushed through her veins like a runaway freight train. Her heart pounded with such intensity she expected it to burst at any moment.

Squeak. The sound startled her. Someone had opened the hall closet.

What was going on? Did she dare peek?

She tilted her head an inch, then another to see past the kitchen doorway. What was she doing? She hated scary movies where the heroine was too stupid to live. Forget this. She'd call for help and let the police take care of her living room guest.

She eased the phone back in the cradle, counted to five and slowly lifted it out again. Never had she been happier to hear a dial tone. She slid down to the floor, hiding in the corner. She kept the knife in front of her for protection if she needed it and dialed 9-1-1.

Erin told the operator someone was in her home and gave her address. Although she whispered, in the dark stillness of the room it sounded like a shout. "Hurry, please."

A crash sounded in the living room, followed by the sound of breaking glass, and then silence.

Had the burglar heard her on the phone? Was he going to come for her? Or had he run away?

Erin's mind counted the seconds. Jack. Tess. She wanted to run down the hall to her family. But what if the burglar heard her and followed? No. They'd be safer if she remained in place. Waiting. Praying. Suddenly red and blue lights from the police car in her driveway poured through the windows and danced across the foyer walls. Only then did she dare leave her hiding place.

Within seconds, she opened the dead bolt and welcomed the officers inside. She flipped on lights in the foyer, living room and kitchen, seeing the scene for the first time. The two officers, with Erin trailing a healthy distance behind, walked through each room. Nothing seemed out of place or disturbed. Erin took a hurried look around and nothing appeared to be missing, either.

"Tell us again what happened, ma'am," one of the police officers asked.

Erin pulled her robe tighter, hugging her arms around her body. "I heard a noise. Someone was in the house. I couldn't call for help from the bedroom, so I had to sneak into the kitchen for the phone. I called 9-1-1. I think he heard me and ran off."

The officers glanced at each other. Everyone turned at the sudden commotion in the foyer.

Tony burst through the door, flashed his badge at the officers and folded her in his arms. "Are you okay? Jack? Tess?"

She welcomed his strength and allowed herself to lean her head against his chest. "We're fine."

"I heard the call go out on the scanner and got here as quickly as I could." He tilted her chin and looked into her eyes. "What happened?"

"Someone broke into the house."

One officer had gone outside. The other stood quietly by their side.

"There are no signs of forced entry, ma'am."

Erin could hear the sound of Tony's heart beating beneath her ear and the strong, steady rhythm comforted her. Slowly, she lifted her face from his chest and turned her attention to the waiting officer.

"I'm sorry. What did you say?"

"There are no signs of forced entry. Did you actually see anyone, ma'am?"

"No. I hid in the kitchen."

"Can you tell me if anything's missing?" The officer held a pen poised over a small notepad and waited for her response.

She stepped away from Tony and wrapped her arms around herself. "It doesn't look like anything has been stolen. But I heard something break."

"Are you sure, ma'am? Take a good look around. Take your time."

Erin did as requested and shook her head.

"Maybe you frightened him off before he could do any damage," the officer said.

"Wait," Erin said. "My aunt's crystal vase. That's what broke."

They looked at the broken pieces of crystal sticking out beneath the table cover.

Tony moved the curtains. "The window's open. Maybe he came in here."

"Or maybe the rustling you heard was a breeze blowing the curtains and it knocked the vase over. See. Nothing to worry about," the officer assured her.

"Unless the wind has size twelve feet." All three heads turned toward the second officer standing in the entranceway. "Found a footprint in the flower bed beneath that window."

Tony had moved to the foyer. "Erin, did you open this closet door?"

"No. But I heard it squeak. I've been meaning to oil it and keep forgetting. I know he opened that door."

Tony withdrew a pen from his pocket and, careful not to disturb any possible prints, he slowly eased the door open all the way.

"What's this?"

Tony grinned and Erin moved closer to see what he found so amusing. In the bottom of the closet was an old army blanket, a flashlight, two comic books, an action figure and a half-eaten peanut butter sandwich.

"That's Jack's fort. He loves playing in there." Erin snatched up the sandwich. "I don't know how many times I've told him not to leave food lying around, especially in Florida, but does he listen? No."

Tony placed his hands on her shoulders and eased her to the side. "What have we here?" He took out a handkerchief, bent down and gingerly lifted a small pile of photographs. He brought them out into the light of the foyer and laid them on the hall table. The grim expression on his face and furious glint in his eyes made a chill race up her spine.

"Tony? What is it?"

Tony turned to one of the police officers. "Call it in. This is a crime scene. We need forensics here stat."

"Tony?" Erin stepped closer for a look at the photographs

splayed across the table top. Her stomach twisted in knots and her legs threatened to collapse. They were photographs of her. At the grocery store. Coming out of work. Sitting on the porch. Playing with Jack in the yard. There were even pictures of her at the Easter picnic fundraiser. And every picture had a black X over her face.

Crouching behind the bushes, he ignored the ache in his legs and stared through the high-powered camera lens at the house. He knew it wasn't safe to be here. The cops were still crawling all over the place. But he was far enough away. They weren't looking for him. They probably thought he'd be long gone by now. And he knew he should be. But he had to see. Had to know if they found the gift he'd left for them in the hall closet. A giggle escaped his lips.

He peered through the lens and brought the scene into focus. There she was. Pacing back and forth on her porch. He'd guessed the commotion had woken the old lady. She was sitting in one of the porch rockers. Her neighbor sat in the other one. He didn't quite know if the man was being neighborly or just plain nosy. Didn't matter. None of them mattered but her.

He moaned in frustration. He didn't have a satisfactory view from here but he didn't dare draw closer.

A smile twisted his lips. He was right. She didn't deserve to be a mother. She locked her boy in the hall closet with comic books and a flashlight. Rage raced through him until he couldn't hold it in anymore and he whined like a hurt, wild animal. He'd make her pay. She'd pay.

He thought about the other women. The store clerk. The secretary. The nurse. He'd punished each of them. He'd made them suffer until they cried for mercy. Until they begged him for death.

He knew he was a hero. Better than any of the plastic super heroes the kids played with. He rescued children from the clutches of evil women. When he had needed a rescuer, waited for a rescuer, begged for a rescuer—no one had come for him. He knew then what he had to do. He had to become the rescuer he had dreamed about. And he did.

He lifted the camera again. Focusing the lens on her face, his breath caught in his throat. He had to remind himself he wasn't on the porch with her. He wasn't close enough to stroke the light touch of rose on her cheeks.

He took deep, calming breaths. *Be patient.* His fingers adjusted the lens. Her eyes drew him into their green depths. Eyes darkened with questions and fear.

She was beautiful, more so than any of the others.

He'd make sure she remained conscious for every second of the exquisite, endless pain he'd bestow upon her.

"Beauty is only skin deep," he whispered into the darkness. No one else could see the black, evil heart within her. The selfishness. The cruelty. But he could. And she'd pay.

He blinked hard. Had the words escaped his lips or were they only within his mind? Had anybody heard? He looked around. No faces coming to neighboring windows to investigate. No porch lights suddenly turned on. His heart stopped hammering. He was safe.

She stepped inside the house. The detective blocked his view. As the minutes passed, his annoyance at not being able to see her grew. He chewed on his lip until he tasted his own blood and fought the urge to venture out of the shadows to pace. Seconds passed. Minutes.

Be patient. It's not time. There's no hurry. No hurry at all.

When she came back into view, she glanced out the window and seemed to look directly at him. He jumped back and then he relaxed. She couldn't see him in the darkness. He was the one with the advantage. His grin broadened.

The woman's face shifted, contorted, features fading in and out of focus. It couldn't be. He pressed against the eyepiece wishing away the image he saw. Mother? Painful cramps seized his stomach muscles. Dropping his camera in the grass, he dry-heaved into the bushes. It's not my mother. A low, animal-like keening filled the night air. *Did that sound come from me?* A second wave of nausea twisted his gut and memories of his childhood bombarded his mind. He trembled with intense hatred.

He tried again to see through the window. He held the camera to his face. *Steady. Steady.* The woman appearing in his camera lens this time wore the softest expression. Innocent. Loving. *Liar. I know what you are.* He moved deeper into the darkness and sat on the ground. *Get hold of yourself. You know she's not your mother, idiot. You killed her with your bare hands. Now calm down and stop acting like a moron.*

"Don't call me a moron!" he hissed into the night, twisting his neck, looking behind him, beside him, searching for the taunting voice. "You don't have to be so mean." Only silence answered.

He raised the lens again and took another look at the scene inside.

See. It's the boy's mother, idiot. Not yours.

He moved farther into the darkness as the woman walked back onto the porch with the man. He patted her shoulder and then bounded down the stairs. She waved goodbye as he hurried down the sidewalk. *Go ahead, fool him but you can't fool me.* He wanted to snatch her and end it now.

Wouldn't it be a delight if he waited for the cops to leave and grabbed her tonight? They wouldn't be expecting it. The thought of making fools out of the police was almost more than he could bear. But he had to wait. There was another child who needed him and he'd already committed himself to help. But he would return. Soon. Very soon.

He wiped sweat from his cheek. Or was it tears? He had waited long enough. It was time.

Tony sat in his car and stared at the brightly lit house. He knew Erin was safe. Police were everywhere. But still he hesitated to leave. He couldn't get her out of his mind. The sweet smell of her breath. The flush of her skin. Her green eyes wide with expectation and something more. Something he didn't want to recognize or admit.

He flashed back to the moment he heard her address coming across the scanner. Adrenaline laced with fear had raced through his blood and remnants of terror caused his pulse to gallop. She could have been killed tonight. This was not a random burglary by a kid high on dope. Erin was a target. And that knowledge took his breath away.

Tony turned the key in the ignition. The last thing in the world he needed was an emotional entanglement with a single mother and her kid. He was a cop, and proud of it, but it's not a job for a family man. Family man? Where had that thought come from? No way. Not him. He slid the car away from the curb.

He had been holding his emotions in check, refusing to get too close, care too much, because someday he might find himself in danger. He never wanted to cause another person that fear or pain. Tony grimaced at the bitter irony of the situation. Who would have believed that Erin would be the one in danger?

A serial killer? Lord, isn't this a lousy way to teach me that cops aren't the only ones who can be in danger? Not that I'm second-guessing You or anything. I know You see the whole picture of our lives and I can only grasp a piece at a time. But, Lord, please help me. How am I supposed to keep this predator away from her door when he has already slipped in right under my nose?

The thought sickened him. He shook his head. Erin. His heart ached thinking about her. She needed him. She needed his expertise. His strength. His protection. She needed him to be the best cop he knew how to be.

But what about his needs? When had those needs started to include her presence in his life? He paused at the Stop sign and looked at Erin's house in his rearview mirror. He had to get out of here. He had to go someplace where he could think straight—and pray.

EIGHT

Jack wrapped his arms around Tony's legs. An instant rush of affection for the boy seized his heart.

"My bike's the greatest. I can ride it all by myself. But Mom won't let me take it outside."

"I will let you take it outside," Erin corrected as she came down the hall and met Tony in the foyer. "Tomorrow morning."

"But I want Tony to see me ride now."

Tony slipped past the child's walker. "Your mom's right, partner. It's going to be dark out there soon."

"Oh-kay. But watch me ride to the kitchen." Jack hurried over to his bike.

"As you can see," Erin said, "your gift is the highlight of his day. But his birthday isn't for another three weeks. Today is Amy's birthday. Don't you think it a little confusing to be giving him his gift so soon? And on Amy's birthday?"

"I gave Amy a big wheel. She'll think I gave Jack the bike so they can ride together and, in a way, that's true. Besides," Tony said, "I remember how upset Jack was about not being able to ride bikes with his school friends." Tony nodded toward the bike. "When one of the guys at work told me about this bike, I couldn't resist taking a look. It's built with three wheels for stability and has a back and straps for extra support for children with his muscle problems. I know it's not a two-wheeler, but he'll be able to ride in the cul-de-sac now with his friends. I thought it important to give it to him before the school year ends so he won't continue to feel excluded."

"Thank you." Erin stood on tiptoe and pressed her lips softly against his. Electricity shot through every nerve ending in his body. He held his breath so tightly his lungs threatened to burst as her fingers caressed the side of his face. He had to muster all the masculine control in his power not to crush her to him and kiss her with the passion and desire he held at bay.

Erin made him feel things he didn't want to feel. She made him think about the possibilities of commitment and family. Even though he'd never had anyone to teach him how, maybe he could learn to be a good dad. His job taught him what *not* to do. Maybe if he did the opposite it would be okay.

Tony gazed into the green depths of her eyes. Maybe he wasn't destined to live alone, to be married to his job. He had never entertained these thoughts before and wasn't sure he wanted to think about them now, but lately they cropped up in his consciousness with regularity. Erin made him feel—hope.

"Beep. Beep. Me, too. Vroom. Vroom."

Tony side-stepped just in time to keep his feet from being flattened by a tiny, blond-haired girl speeding past on a Big Wheel.

"That's Amy. What can I say? Your gift was a hit with her, too. Enter at your own risk, Mr. Detective." Erin laughed and the deep, throaty sound made him smile. "Things are pretty wild here today. If you can make it to the kitchen in one piece, the adults are hiding out in there."

Tony hung his jacket on a hook by the door and followed Erin's lead. The aroma of roast beef and fresh coffee teased his nostrils and reminded his empty, rumbling stomach just how hungry he was.

"There's the lad," Tess announced and cleared a spot for him. "What's your poison?"

"How can I resist your Irish coffee, Tess? No one makes a better brew." He sat and nodded a greeting to both Patrick and Carol.

"Hello, Mr. Fitzgerald. Nice to meet you again."

"I don't call meeting during that horrible incident two nights ago a real introduction. You can call me Pat or Fitz. Just don't call me late for dinner." The man's grip was stronger than Tony expected. The old man's gaze followed Tess about the room. Tony knew there was more afoot here than just being a neighbor.

"Hello, Carol."

"Nice to see you again, Tony. The way we met is a memory I plan to keep for a long time. It isn't every day I get to witness my best friend mortified."

Tony laughed. He found her friendliness and honesty refreshing and took an instant liking to her.

"Thank you for the gift for Amy. That was generous and unexpected," Carol said.

As if on cue, Amy slammed her Big Wheel into the leg of the table and the adults scrambled to save their cups from spilling.

"Amy, honey, watch what you're doing," Carol gently scolded her daughter.

"I'm dwiving, Mama."

"I see that, sweetheart, but it's time for dinner." Carol lifted the child to her lap, kissed her blond curls, then settled her into the booster seat beside her. "Driving is for outside play."

"You have an adorable daughter, Carol," Tony said.

Carol returned his smile. "Thank you. She is, isn't she?"

"I want to sit next to Tony." Jack climbed up on the empty chair to Tony's left.

"Hope you brought a healthy appetite," Tess said.

"To your house? I've been starving myself all day in anticipation of the best cooking in town."

Tess blushed and everyone chuckled.

Roast beef, mashed potatoes, green bean casserole, biscuits and two slices of birthday cake later, Tony leaned back and groaned with satisfaction. The past hour had been filled with the sound of children's voices, laughter and good conversation. He'd watched the interactions around the table with interest. All this touchy-feely family stuff was not good for his self-preservation. He'd lived quite well through the years without the idea of a family of his own ever crossing his mind. He wanted to keep it that way. Didn't he?

Erin and Carol excused themselves to prepare the children for bed. Patrick stood up, thanked Tess for a fabulous meal, leaned close to Tony's ear and whispered, "If you know what's good for you, you'll make your getaway, too. Carol's going out tonight and the other two are planning to watch a chick flick."

"I hear you, old man." Tess turned from the sink and stared him down. "*Jerry Maguire* is not a chick flick. It's about a sports agent. Since when is a football movie considered a chick flick?"

Patrick stood his ground. "Football movie my Irish…"

"Watch your language in this house." Tess planted her fists on her hips and feigned anger but amusement glittered in her eyes and teased the corners of her mouth.

Patrick looked back at Tony. "They say it's about football so poor, dumb fools like me agree to sit down and watch it. I made that mistake years ago when the movie first came out." He waved his hand in the air.

Tess slapped Patrick's arm with a dish towel. "Go away with you now. Coming here and sampling my fine cookin' and then putting down the entertainment I picked."

Patrick clasped Tess's hand and planted a kiss on the back of it. "The cooking was fine, indeed. That it was." He headed for the back door and just before he left, he looked over his shoulder at Tony and yelled, "Run, son. Don't say I didn't warn you."

Tess threw the dish towel, but it hit a closed door.

Tony laughed, grabbed a clean towel from the drawer and helped Tess finish the dishes while Erin and Carol put the children to bed. He was putting the last dish away when Erin returned. Wisps of hair escaped her fasteners and curled against her skin. The natural rosy glow of her cheeks created a beauty that didn't require makeup. His heart skipped a beat at the sight of her. She moved toward him with lightness and confidence. He found it increasingly difficult to take his eyes off her.

"Jack's already asleep." She smiled at him and his pulse thundered against his wrists.

Tony placed a cup of coffee on the table in front of her.

"I drink too much coffee, but thanks." She took a sip. "I'm going to turn into a coffee urn."

"It would be the prettiest coffee urn I've ever seen." He grinned when a fresh rush of color tinged her cheeks. Boy, he loved teasing her.

"Amy's down for the count, too." Carol's voice sounded from the doorway. She had changed clothes and now wore a simple but flattering black silk dress. Her blond hair hung loosely on her shoulders. She was a strikingly pretty woman, Tony thought, but she couldn't hold a candle to Erin's natural beauty.

"I wish you'd tell me who you're meeting," Erin said. "It's not like you to keep secrets from me."

"I know. I just want to be sure this is going where I think it is before I bring him home to family and friends."

"Must be serious," Erin said.

Carol's voice grew wistful. "This could be the love of my

life…for the rest of my life." Carol frowned. "Are you sure you don't mind Amy spending the night?"

"How can you even ask? You know how much I love that little girl."

"I know. But—" she glanced at Tony, smiled sheepishly and looked back at Erin "—I thought you might have plans of your own for the evening."

Erin laughed and nudged her friend toward the door. "Wake me when you get home. I don't care what time it is. I want to hear every detail."

Carol hugged Erin. "I won't be out too late." Glancing his way, she smiled, said good-night and left.

Tony joined Erin at the table and gestured toward the empty doorway. "Something wrong?"

"No, I guess not. But the secrecy bothers me. She's dated before and always fills me in. I don't understand why this one is such a Mystery Man."

"Maybe because this one matters."

Erin raised an eyebrow.

"The relationship is new. Fragile. Exciting. Maybe she's not ready to share what they've found with the world just yet." He kept his voice low, steady, trying not to reveal what effect her nearness was having on him. He didn't want to ruin the moment. But he didn't know how much longer he could be the perfect friend, the shoulder for her to cry on, without wanting more. And more was the last thing he could let himself want.

"Maybe. But I'm getting the goods when she gets home tonight if I have to sit on her until she spills her guts."

"Wish I knew earlier how you respond to secrets. I would have kept one or two myself."

Erin lowered her head, but not before he saw a smile pull at her lips.

"Don't mind me. I'm just an invisible fly on the wall over here," Tess said. "I'll just take myself into the living room and set up our 'chick flick' for tonight. That is, of course, if the two of you are inclined to join me." Tess took off her apron and paused in the doorway, a devilish glint in her eye. "You know, it's the oddest thing. The oven's been off for hours but the heat in this room is unbelievable." Her chuckles followed her down the hall.

Tony's expression made Erin pause. He was deep in thought, eyebrows furrowed together, chewing on his lower lip.

"Something wrong?"

"What did you say Carol's last name is?" Tony asked.

"Henderson. Why?"

"No reason." He rubbed his hand through his hair like she'd seen him do a hundred times before when something puzzled him. "I know that name."

"You met her at the Easter fundraiser. And I talk about her all the time."

"True. But you don't use her full name. You just refer to her as Carol or Amy's mom. I'm not sure you ever mentioned her last name before, did you?"

Erin wore a puzzled expression. "I really don't know. Does it matter?"

"Carol Henderson. Her name's nagging at me. I've heard it, but I can't place it." He shrugged. "It'll come to me." He stood up and offered his hand. "We'd better go. Tess is waiting for us and I have it on good authority that this is a movie I don't want to miss."

"Really?" Erin placed her hand in his and stood. "You like romance movies?" She couldn't keep the surprise out of her voice.

"Shh," Tony whispered, drawing her close. "I love romance

movies. But you can't say a word. It would ruin my tough-guy reputation and I'd have to take drastic measures to keep you silent."

"Really? What drastic measures?"

He claimed her mouth with a kiss filled with so many promises that Erin was sure she'd never be able to speak again.

The next day

"Fwoot Loops," Amy said, holding up her cereal bowl.

"Froot Loops it is." Erin settled the child in the booster chair and filled her bowl.

"Me, too," Jack said.

"Startin' a child off first thing in the morning with a bowl full of sugar is asking for trouble," Tess said as she entered the kitchen. "They have enough energy as it is without spoon-feeding them more." She waved a hand in the air. "I know, I know. Nobody asked me." Tess sat at the table.

"Good morning, Tess." Erin chuckled and poured herself a bowl of the colorful cereal.

"I only see three bowls." Tess sipped some juice. "Aren't we missing somebody?"

Erin laughed. "Carol's probably still sleeping. I didn't hear her come in last night, so it must have been late. I decided to let her sleep in."

"I'm sure she'll thank you for the few extra hours of shut-eye." Tess folded her arms on the table. "I'm glad you and Tony had a nice time last night. I say it's high time you started showing a little interest in the lad. I think he's quite a catch." She raised her hand to ward off any censure. "I know. It doesn't matter what I think. It's your life."

Erin leaned closer to her aunt and lowered her voice so the

children wouldn't hear their conversation. "Tess, the more I try to keep him out of my thoughts, the more he's the star attraction. We both know he's a great guy. And he's good-looking, too."

"Terrible things to say about the lad. Just terrible."

Erin ignored her aunt's teasing barb. "I don't know where I want the relationship to go. I haven't been in a serious relationship since Jack's father. We both know how that turned out."

"Relationship? Lass, you haven't been on a serious date. I've been wondering what it was going to take for you to remember you're a healthy, young woman and not just a mom," Tess whispered.

Erin leaned closer. "He kissed me last night."

"Did he, now?" Tess grinned. "Was it a good kiss?"

Erin's cheeks flooded with warmth. She looked directly into her aunt's eyes. "It was a please-don't-stop-I'm-melting-right-into-the-floor kiss."

"I had me one of them melting kisses once," Tess said. "I've been kissing everything that moves ever since looking for another."

Both women laughed out loud.

"Tess, it was like something you read about in fairy tales. It scared me to death."

"Scared you? Why?"

Erin struggled to find the right words. "When I'm with Tony, I don't feel in control of my life. I feel vulnerable and uncertain."

"Control? Is that what you want? A neat little life where everything's predictable?" Tess reached across and clasped Erin's hands. "But life isn't neat and tidy, now, is it? There's laughin' and loving. Disappointments. Tears. The best you can hope is to have faith and ask God to give you the strength to survive life's ups and downs. But control?" Tess chuckled. "My mother used to say, 'You plan and God laughs.'"

Jack pulled on his mother's sleeve. "Mom, can we go play now?"

"Did you eat all your cereal?"

"Uh-huh," Amy said, the last mouthful of cereal garbling her speech.

"Okay." She lifted Amy off the chair. "But don't make a mess."

"We won't," they chorused and scurried away.

"We can learn a lot from those sweet children," Tess said. "They're filled with such joy and energy." Tess patted Erin's hand. "*Live* your life, child. Time is a thief and life passes before you know it."

"So you think I should take a chance with Tony?"

Tess rolled her eyes. "Haven't you heard a word I've been saying?"

"Okay, Tess." Erin laughed and gestured for her to stop. "I get the picture."

"I've been thinking," Tess said. "I'll be visitin' that nice Mr. Fitzgerald after dinner tonight. We've been flirtin' over the backyard fence long enough. It's about time I find out if he can melt one into the floorboards."

Erin's eyes widened.

"Don't look at me like that," Tess fussed. "I'm still breathing, aren't I?"

Both women laughed and continued to enjoy their morning coffee.

NINE

Tony gestured to the chair beside his desk. "Have a seat." He scrutinized the man, tall, clean-cut, expensive suit and shoes. *And wanting to be anywhere else but here.* "I'm Detective Marino. How can I help you, Mr…?"

"Dr. Robert Stone." The man squirmed in his chair. "This is incredibly awkward."

Tony waited, knowing silence was a powerful interrogation technique.

"I'm probably being foolish," Stone said. "I'm sure nothing's wrong."

Everything about the man's demeanor screamed otherwise. Tony smiled encouragement but remained silent.

"My date didn't meet me last night. I've called her multiple times, even drove to her home, but she wasn't there."

Before Tony could respond, Stone said, "I know it sounds juvenile but Carol wouldn't stand me up. She knew I was planning something special. She just wouldn't have done that."

The name caught Tony's attention. "Carol?"

"Carol Henderson."

"She's a nurse at the hospital?" Tony tensed.

Dr. Stone raised an eyebrow. "Yes, do you know her?"

"I met her recently." Tony picked up a pen. "You say you had a special date?"

"Yes. We were supposed to meet at eight o'clock at the gazebo beside the Granada Bridge."

"If the date was special, why meet her? Why didn't you pick her up?"

Dr. Stone shifted in his seat. "She spent the day with friends. It was easier to agree to meet."

Tony's suspicions grew. Something more was going on here. He'd been lied to by the best and this guy wasn't one of them.

The doctor lowered his gaze. "Carol spent the day with her best friend, Erin O'Malley."

Tony leaned back in his seat. "Have you called to check if she's seen Carol?"

Stone looked at his hands. "I was hoping you might do that."

Tony arched an eyebrow. "Why's that?"

"I used to date Ms. O'Malley. I'd find it awkward asking her about Carol."

He dated Erin? Hmm, he hadn't seen that coming.

"We didn't part on the best of terms," the doctor continued. "Although I've run into Erin a few times since the breakup and it seems to be water under the bridge, still..." Stone shrugged. "I don't think Carol told her we were dating."

Tony studied him with new interest. *Was Erin still harboring feelings for this man? Why did it end badly? And who ended it?*

"Why's that? Is Carol the kind of person who would date someone her best friend still cared about?" Tony asked.

"Of course not." Stone straightened in his chair. Obviously outraged at the question, he glared at Tony. "Carol was a wonderful human being. And fiercely loyal to the people she loved." He shook his head. "She was certain Erin was finished with me long before we started dating. It was my feelings for Erin she questioned."

Tony tented his fingers against his lips and rocked back in his chair. Thoughts ricocheted through his mind like a fired pinball. After a moment, he sat upright. "You said 'was.'"

Stone looked puzzled.

"You said Carol 'was' a sweet human being. Do you have any reason to believe she still isn't, Doctor?"

The man sputtered. "No, of course not, I…"

Tony waited.

Tears welled up in the doctor's eyes. He pulled a small velvet box from his pocket and flipped it open to reveal a stunning diamond ring. "I planned to propose. Carol wouldn't have stood me up. Something had to happen to her."

Tony poured the doctor a glass of water. "Did Carol know your plans?"

"We've had several general discussions. About marriage. About children." Stone sipped his water before continuing. "Truthfully, Detective, I'm so in love with the woman I don't know how she couldn't know."

Surprised by the man's show of raw emotion, Tony softened his voice. "Do you have any specific reason to believe something happened to Ms. Henderson? I understand not meeting you for your date was unlike her. But is there anything else I should know?"

Dr. Stone's shoulders slumped forward. He looked defeated and weary. "Carol's been receiving anonymous phone calls. She filed a police report a couple of weeks ago."

The hair on the back of Tony's neck stood up. That's why Carol's name had been so familiar. He'd overheard Spence telling Winters he was going to check it out to see if there might be any connection to their victims. They'd discovered all the victims had received calls, but the information hadn't been obvious because some of the women had reported it to the sheriff's office and others reported it to their local police department.

The doctor's eyes darkened, anger evident in his voice. "Then she started receiving anonymous packages. Rotten fruit. Dead flowers. All accompanied by threatening notes. The last box contained pictures of Carol with her head cut out of the pictures. She reported it to the police." Stone rubbed his eyes, lack of sleep evident on his face. "Your department took it seriously. Unfortunately, they said there wasn't enough evidence for them to arrest anyone. They would continue to investigate and hoped to produce a lead. Meanwhile, they warned her to be cautious where she went and who she spoke to. Now she's missing."

Tony held his head in his hands. His stomach twisted. Carol's image, Amy's laughing face and Erin's smile all spiraled through his mind. He prayed for strength, for wisdom. How was he going to tell Erin that he believed her best friend had become a victim of a serial killer? And that his gut told him she was next?

Erin heard the crunch of gravel and looked up from watering the plants to see her aunt approach. "Hi. Where are the kids?"

"Watching a video in the living room. Still no word from Carol?" Tess asked.

"No, and I'm worried. I was concerned when I knocked on her door this morning and found she hadn't come home last night. But now I don't know what to think. No matter how much fun she had last night, she would have at least called by now. You know how protective she is about Amy."

"I know. I'm worried, too. Maybe we should call someone."

"Who would I call? She's not scheduled to work. She's not

answering her cell. I don't know who this 'Mystery Man' is."
Erin stooped down and wound up the hose. "Why did she have
to be so secretive? I can't believe she's been seeing this guy
for months and the first I hear about it is Amy's birthday
party." Frustration laced her words. "Now I don't have a clue
where to start looking for her."

"Maybe we should call the police."

Erin stood and pulled off her gardening gloves. "And tell
them what? That she left last night looking like a million
bucks to go on a special date and we haven't seen her since?
Somehow, I don't think they'll be too concerned."

"Well, we have to do something. We can't just sit here."

Erin sighed. "That's exactly what we have to do. Until she
calls or shows up or something."

They both heard the doorbell.

"I'll get it," Erin said. "Why don't you go inside and check
on the kids?" She hurried around the side of the house,
shielded her eyes against the sun and grinned when she recognized the man on the porch. "Hi. I wasn't expecting you."

Tony came down the steps. His grave expression as he approached gave her pause.

*Tell me nothing's wrong. Tell me I have a vivid imagi-
nation and you came by to see me...or Jack...or that you're
here for some Irish coffee.*

"What's wrong?" she asked.

"Have you heard from Carol?"

Erin's stomach clenched. "No. Why?" She shoved her
hands in her pockets to still the sudden trembling in them.

"When was the last time you spoke with her?"

"Last night. Right before she left for her date. But you
know that already. You were here." She took a deep breath.
"Tony, what's going on? You're scaring me."

"She's missing."

"I know that, but how did you…?" An uneasy feeling crept over her. "What's happened?"

He slid a protective arm around her shoulders and gently guided her toward the house. "As far as I know, nothing's happened to her. Let's go inside and talk."

They no sooner stepped into the foyer than the children raced toward them, hugging Tony's legs and shouting his name.

"Tony, are you going to watch me ride my bike?" Jack asked.

"Me, too," Amy demanded.

Tony squatted and closed both children in a bear hug. "I'd love to play with you guys," he said, an unfamiliar gruffness in his voice. "But it'll have to wait until next time. I have to go back to work in a few minutes."

The gentle way Tony brushed the curls out of Amy's eyes made Erin's heart constrict so tightly that she could barely breathe. *He knows something and it's bad. It's very, very bad.*

"Aunt Tess is going to take you outside," Erin said.

Her aunt nodded and, for once, didn't ask any questions. "Come on, children. Let's go next door and show Mr. Fitzpatrick how well you ride."

After they left, Erin looked at Tony. She didn't want to see sympathy or concern in his eyes, but she did. "Just tell me." She steeled herself for his words.

He tugged her hand and led her into the kitchen. "Someone filed a missing person report earlier today. Normally, we wait forty-eight hours, but under the circumstances, I thought it wouldn't hurt to do a little poking around."

"Someone reported her missing?" She clenched her fists against her chest. *Breathe. One. Two. In. Out.* "I don't understand. Who?"

"The man she was supposed to meet last night."

Erin sat perfectly still. "You met Mystery Man?"

Tony nodded.

"Who is he?"

"That's not important right now."

Erin popped out of her seat. "What do you mean it's not important? If he was the last one to see her, he has to know what happened. Maybe they fought. Maybe he did something to her and he is trying to cover his tracks."

Tony stood, crossed to the sink and got her a glass of water. "Here, drink this."

She pushed it away.

He gently pushed her back into her seat and placed the glass on the table beside her.

"Did he hurt her, Tony? Did he?"

Tony squatted in front of her and cradled her hands in his. "He claims she never showed up. He got worried when she didn't return his calls."

"She never made it to their date? Do you believe him?" Erin pinned him with her gaze.

"Until I have reason to think otherwise, yes, I do."

Erin contemplated his answer and nodded.

Tony took a seat beside her. "Did you know Carol received anonymous telephone calls?"

"Yes." When she saw his features darken, she said, "I was going to tell you about it last night but I forgot. For one wonderful evening I got lost in good food, good conversation and a good movie. I just didn't think about the calls." She crinkled her forehead. "What do the calls have to do with anything?"

"Maybe nothing. What can you tell me about them?"

Erin found the even tone in his voice soothing and his calmness contagious.

"Carol got some prank calls just about the same time I started getting them and changed her number. They stopped for a while. But recently they started up again. Worse this time. He started whispering terrible things. She got upset and reported them to the police."

Tony took a small notepad out of his pocket. "Anything else?"

"She started getting weird, disgusting gifts. Rotten fruit, dead bugs, creepy stuff. She reported all of it and although the cops seemed concerned, there didn't seem to be much they could do about it." Erin stared at him. "Please tell me you don't think this has anything to do with her disappearance."

"I'm not sure of anything right now. I'm just trying to cover all the angles." He scribbled in his pad. "Can you think of anyone that might want to hurt Carol? Anyone mad at her? Holding a grudge?"

"Of course not." Erin thought for a moment and then said, "Except… This is silly. It couldn't possibly have anything to do with Carol's disappearance."

Tony encouraged her with a smile. "Why don't you tell me anyway? You never know what might be helpful."

Erin fidgeted with her hands. "Carol didn't get along with Lenny, one of the lab technicians at the hospital. Truthfully, she was uncharacteristically harsh with the man. She believed he was the one making the calls."

Tony held his pen over the notepad. "Do you have a last name for Lenny?"

"Richards. But Lenny couldn't have had anything to do with this. He's…well, a little odd…a loner…doesn't seem to know how to make friends. But I can't believe he'd ever hurt anyone. I never did believe he made those calls."

"Why not?"

"I don't know." Erin shrugged. "Female intuition? Lenny's

like an ugly old dog that gets kicked around a lot. He licks his wounds, growls sometimes but he doesn't bite back."

Tony tucked the notebook back in his suit pocket and stood.

Erin's throat muscles tightened. She forced herself to speak. "Do you think the calls have something to do with Carol's disappearance?"

He shrugged. "It's just a piece of the puzzle. Probably nothing. Your calls stopped, didn't they?"

She hesitated.

"Erin?" Tony impaled her with his eyes.

"I've been getting them again for the past few days."

"Why didn't you tell me?"

She winced at the anger evident in his expression. "You've been busy with the case you're working on. I filed a formal complaint. I just didn't get around to mentioning it to you. I guess I just hoped they'd go away."

Tony sighed heavily. "Erin, I need you to tell me *every-thing*. I can't help you if I don't know what's going on."

"You think these calls are significant, don't you? What aren't you telling me?" She pinned him with her eyes and wouldn't let him look away.

"*All* of the victims in the case I'm investigating received similar calls. Carol got calls and she's missing. That's a strong enough coincidence not to disregard anything."

Erin ducked her head. Her stomach somersaulted and a wave of dizziness threatened to drop her.

Tony gently kneaded her shoulders. "I have to get back to work. Are you going to be all right?"

"Sure." She took comfort in his tenderness and concern.

"Erin, right now I need you to do what I ask. No arguments. No debates. Do you think you can do that?"

She nodded.

"Let your answering machine screen all your calls. And if you hear from Carol, call me immediately. You know how to reach me 24/7. You have my home, work and cell numbers. Use them." He tilted her chin. "Keep the house locked both day and night. And don't go anywhere alone." He trailed his index finger down her cheek. "Promise?"

"I promise."

"Now walk me out and lock the door behind me." When he reached the door, she called his name and he looked back. The tears she'd been fighting flowed in silent rivulets down her cheeks. "Bring Carol home, Tony. Please. Bring her home."

TEN

Sergeant Greene slammed his hand on the table. "I'm not letting this lunatic get away with it again." He paced the front of the room. "Marino, when did this woman go missing?"

"She was last seen seven-thirty Sunday night."

The sergeant wrote the time on the board in the front of the room. "She's been missing less than thirty-two hours. He doesn't kill them right away. This one may still be alive."

"What do we know about her?" He poised his marker over the board.

"Same age range." Spence consulted his notes. "Walks out the door for a specific destination and vanishes into thin air. No witnesses. No signs of struggle."

Sergeant Greene nodded, wrote the name *Carol Henderson* beside the other victims and added *same age, no witnesses, no signs of struggle* to the column.

"Winters, what did you find out about the boyfriend?"

"Stone's clean. Not even a traffic ticket," Winters said.

Tony stared at Carol's name on the board beside the other victims and bile backed up in his throat. The lab tech, Lenny, had been his one viable lead and an ironclad alibi took that off the table. Now he was back to square one. No suspects.

No leads. How could this be happening? This was hitting too close to home.

"Okay, let's review," Sarge said. All four men stared at the pictures taped to the board. "What do we know about these women?"

"Neighbors and friends all reported the victims seemed out of sorts, nervous, shortly before they disappeared," Winters said.

"That's right. I've confirmed that all of our victims received anonymous telephone calls. We didn't pick up on it right away because the reports were filed in different jurisdictions and the communications on prank calls fell through the cracks." Spence took a sip of his coffee and then grimaced at its bitterness.

"Make it four," Spence said. "I've confirmed Carol Henderson filed a complaint with the Holly Hill police."

The blood drained out of Tony's face. This couldn't be happening. *The victims got calls. Carol got calls. Please, God, don't let anything happen to Erin.*

"Make it five." Tony looked directly at his sergeant. "Erin O'Malley, a friend of mine, is receiving calls. She's Carol's best friend."

"This is the first solid lead we've had. I want a trap put on her line today. Winters, you handle it." Sarge paused while he digested the new information. "So the killer likes to taunt his victims before he grabs them. We can hand that to the press. What other angle can we explore?" The sergeant tapped the marker on the board. "The answer's here, men. We're just not seeing it."

"They're all single mothers," Spence said.

"Not all. Cynthia Mayors was married," Winters corrected.

"Newlywed," Spence said. "A quickie wedding in Vegas and the guy ships off to Iraq. Maybe the killer didn't know she got married. Maybe he thought she was still a single mom."

"What about it, Marino? Is your friend a single mom?"

Tony nodded.

"Okay," Sarge said. "Let's play with that angle. The guy doesn't like single mothers. There are millions of single parents out there. What makes these four special?"

"The kids." Tony's voice raised an octave with excitement.

"News flash. All single mothers have kids," Spence said.

"Not just kids. Special kids. Look." Tony raced up to the board and pointed at each name. "Each family has a handicapped kid. Mayors had two kids, one of them autistic. Leigh Porter has four children, the second child is deaf. Carol's child has Down syndrome."

"Anne Morton's kid isn't handicapped," Spence said.

"Wait a minute." Winters quickly paged through his notebook. "The Morton kid is in regular third grade classes, but when I interviewed her teacher, she told me the child had a specific learning disability. She gets extra tutoring and occupational and physical therapy twice a week."

Tony stared at the board in disbelief. "That's it. That's the connection." *Erin. Single mom. Handicapped child. Anonymous calls.* "Erin O'Malley's son has cerebral palsy. Erin's our next target."

"Are you all right, Marino?" Sarge asked.

"Fine, sir."

His sergeant stared at him like he was a bug under a microscope. "Just how good a friend is this woman?"

Tony hesitated. He knew Erin was going to hate police poking around in her life. He also knew the sergeant might remove him from the case if he felt Tony was in over his head. The job had always been first, last and always with him. There'd never been a question where his duty lay until now. A picture of Erin entered his mind. Her short auburn curls catching the sunlight. Her green eyes shining with intelligence and challenge. Her lips soft and full. She was in danger. His duty was to protect her, no matter the cost. He offered up a silent prayer that neither Erin nor the sergeant would cut him out of the loop.

"I met both Carol Henderson and Erin O'Malley at the Easter parade three weeks ago. I had dinner with both women at Ms. O'Malley's home last night. Based on what we know about this man, I believe Erin O'Malley is on his list of victims, possibly his next victim." He looked the sergeant straight in the eye. "And that makes it personal for me, sir. Very personal."

The sergeant stared intently at him.

Tony paused before asking, "Will you be removing me from the case, sir?"

"Are you going to give me a reason to remove you, Marino? Will your personal involvement with this woman impede your ability to investigate this case?"

"No, sir." Tony fought to hide his relief.

The sergeant nodded and Tony returned to his seat.

"All right, men. I know we've interviewed every hospital employee and come up with nothing. Interview them again. We need to go deeper. We found a connection. Find out every place these women have ever taken their kids. I want to know and I want to know it yesterday. What school do they attend? What park do they play in? What babysitters do they use? Where do they shop? Where do they fill their medications? What doctors do they use? Carol Henderson is missing, men. Missing. Not dead yet. What are you waiting for? Go!" The men stood to leave. "Marino, give me a minute."

Tony joined the sergeant in the front of the room. He was surprised to see empathy in the sergeant's eyes. "As you know, I don't have the budget or the manpower to provide Ms.

O'Malley with 24/7 protection. Especially since we're not even sure she's the next target."

Tony nodded. "Understood."

"But I will authorize an increased police presence in her neighborhood. Intermittent, unscheduled drivebys that may throw off anyone who is watching her place."

"Thank you, sir."

The sergeant cleared his voice. "Make sure Ms. O'Malley understands the gravity of her position. See if you can get her to leave town, go visit relatives or something. And if you want to remain on this case, you keep me in a close loop on this one."

"I will, sir. Thank you."

Tony left the building, slid behind the wheel of his car, and slipped his key in the ignition. What was he going to do? He had to find Carol before it was too late. But he was torn. Someone was targeting people he knew, people he cared about. And right now Erin appeared to be at the top of the list. His jaw clenched with determination. He had to find Carol. And he had to find a way to protect Erin. The question was how?

"I'll have the tuna salad on rye with lettuce, tomato and pickle. Gimme potato salad and beans as my sides, a can of Coke and a chocolate chip cookie." Patrick Fitzgerald finished his order, nodded to Tony and left the line to find a table. Tony placed his order, paid for the two lunches and joined the older man.

"This deli has the best box lunches in town," Patrick said. "Thanks for inviting me."

"My pleasure." Tony took a bite of his sandwich.

Patrick took his time spreading a napkin on his lap. "Is this table okay? I got the one closest to the back. Away from everybody. After all, I'm sure what you are about to ask me is private and confidential. You won't want all the other patrons listening in."

Tony, surprised by the elderly man's insight, paused. "What gave me away?"

Patrick chuckled. "I didn't get to be seventy, son, without developing a strong power of observation and some good old common sense. My common sense tells me that a detective I've met twice, once at a child's birthday dinner and then at a break-in, isn't asking me out to lunch because he missed my company. My power of observation tells me you're smitten with our Erin. You want to pump me for information." The old man sat back in his chair and grinned.

"You are observant, Mr. Fitzgerald." Tony smiled.

"Now spit it out. What do you want to know? Or maybe I can save you the trouble. Erin and her family have lived next door to me for the past four years. Erin used to go out with some doctor fellow, but no one lately. She's a great gal, a good mother and deserves to get herself hitched to a good guy. That boy of hers is the smartest little whip I've ever met. And I'm sure your power of observation told you that I have a sweet spot for Tess."

Tony chuckled. "Well, you come right to the point, don't you?"

Patrick nodded. "Only way to be. So what do you want, son? You want me to put in a good word with Erin? I've already done that a time or two, but I'll be happy to do it again."

Tony gestured toward the food. "Please. Enjoy your meal."

The man didn't need a second invitation. He bit into his sandwich with gusto and actually smacked his lips. His facial expression was one of pure delight. "I love this place. Don't get to come here often. The quality of the food and the smells of fresh meats and pickles remind me of the old-fashioned delis when I was a kid. I don't drive too much anymore. Go to the doctor's and the pharmacy and grocery store, but that's all within a couple of miles of my house. So this is a real treat."

"If I'm not being too personal," Tony asked. "How are things going with you and Tess?"

"Better than you and Erin." The man chuckled and took a swig of his drink.

"Do you see Tess often?" Tony asked.

"I manage to pop in once or twice a week. And she pops over to my place now and again. Just because we've got a little snow on the roof doesn't mean we don't play the same courting games you kids do." Patrick grinned.

"So, Tess wouldn't find it unusual behavior if you popped in every day or stayed for longer visits?" Tony finished the last of his lunch, pushed his plate aside and folded his hands on the table.

"No, I suppose not. She might even welcome it if she thought I was doing some matchmaking for you. She's taken a shine to you, you know."

Tony sighed deeply. "Mr. Fitzgerald, I wish that was all I was asking."

Patrick's grin faded. He gulped down the rest of his drink and stacked the empty plates. He sat back in his chair and looked Tony straight in the eye. "What's this all about?"

"Mr. Fitzgerald—"

"Fitz."

"Sorry. Fitz. What I'm about to tell you is confidential. You can't mention this conversation to anyone, not even Tess. Do you think you can keep things quiet?"

"If you have to ask, you've taken the wrong old man to lunch."

Tony smiled and nodded. He leaned forward, lowered his voice and told the man everything. He noticed a slight tremor in the old man's hands, but his stoic expression and calm, level voice told him he had not misjudged him.

"How can I help? What do you want me to do?" Patrick asked.

"Not much more than what you're already doing. I want you to stop by as often as possible. Keep alert to anything unusual, no matter how trivial, and let me know about it. I've already spoken to both Erin and Tess. They know our victims received anonymous calls. They also know that each victim had a handicapped child."

The blood drained from Patrick's face but he remained calm.

"Carol fit the victim's profile. So does Erin. Both Erin and Tess have assured me they'll be on guard for anything out of the ordinary." Tony drew a business card out of his wallet. "This is the number to my cell phone. Call me any hour, night or day."

Patrick accepted the business card and slipped it into his pocket.

"My sergeant is being kept in the loop. Although we don't have the manpower for 24/7 surveillance, there will be an increased police presence patrolling your street. But I need more. I need to have eyes and ears inside the house when I can't be there myself."

Patrick nodded. "I understand." He closed his eyes and slightly bowed his head for a moment as though in silent prayer.

Tony gave Patrick time to process the information and glanced around the room. The cash register dinged. The sound of laughter and conversation drifted from neighboring tables. A young boy running in the aisle accidentally bounced off the edge of their table on the way to the restroom. Everything seemed so normal and uncomplicated. So why did his stomach feel like he had swallowed a burning iron ball?

"Funny thing, this life of ours," Patrick said. "Each day

slips into another until thousands of days have passed. But you still think you have forever." He pulled a handkerchief from his pocket and dabbed moist eyes. "You think you can fall in love, maybe even marry and you'll just keep on ticking like a Timex watch. For a moment, you forget that you're not in charge, God is." Patrick shoved the handkerchief in his pocket and stood. "We've been here long enough, son. Let's head home. We've got work to do."

ELEVEN

Erin barely felt the light breeze on her face, barely noticed the thick cotton ball clouds on this bright sunny day as she sat on the porch and watched the children play. She was merely going through the motions. She answered when someone spoke to her. But her mind wandered and her heart filled with anxiety.

Tess thumped down a glass of iced tea on the side table between the rockers.

Erin jumped. "You startled me. I didn't hear you come out."

"Sorry, lass. But I don't think you would have heard a freighter with a fog horn."

Erin sighed heavily. "You're probably right."

The two women sat side by side, their rockers moving in a unified slow, steady rhythm.

"The children are having a good time," Tess said. "Jack has taken to that bike like it's a second pair of legs." She folded her hands in her lap. "And Amy adores Jack. Follows him everywhere, she does."

Erin smiled.

"Good afternoon, ladies." Patrick sauntered across the lawn and lowered himself to the top porch step. "Mind if I join you for a spell?"

"Since when have you needed an invitation?" Tess admonished. "But I think your old bones might feel better in one of these chairs."

"Old bones. That they are. But I know what you're doing." He rose and pulled a brown wicker chair next to her. "You're flirting with me."

"Me? Flirting with you? I think you have it backward, old man. 'Tis you who's been over here every day this week." Tess tried to sound harsh, but the color in her cheeks and the twinkle in her eye revealed how happy she was to see him.

"Mr. Fitzgerald, look at me." Jack raced his bike down the driveway, across the sidewalk and turned around in Mr. Fitzgerald's driveway before pedaling back. Amy followed in hot pursuit on her Big Wheel.

Patrick waved at the children as they sped past. "Great job, Jack. You, too, Amy." He continued watching and waving for a minute or two before turning his attention back to the women. "How's the little one doing?"

"She's holdin' up pretty good," Tess said. "Still asks for her mother but not as much as the first couple of days." Tess gripped the arms of the chair and rocked.

Patrick nodded.

"She doesn't understand why her mommy doesn't come back and I haven't been able to find a way to explain it to her." Tess rocked faster.

Patrick reached out and put his hand on the arm of the rocker. "Slow down or this chair will hop off this porch and follow the kid's bikes down the street."

Tess slowed her rhythm.

"Erin?" Patrick didn't speak again until she looked at him. "How are you holding up?"

Instantly, tears burned the back of her eyes and blurred her vision. *How am I? My best friend, the person who's been by my side since I was Jack's age, has simply vanished. How am I? I'm dying inside. I can't eat. I can't sleep. I can barely get through a day.*

"I'm fine, Patrick." She forced herself to smile.

Patrick nodded. "They'll find her."

Erin swallowed the sob that threatened to choke her. "Four days." Her voice was little more than a raspy whisper. "She's been missing four days."

Patrick sighed deeply. "Have you seen Tony lately?"

Erin shook her head. "He stopped by a couple of nights ago. But he's working almost around the clock trying to find Carol."

Patrick nodded as he absorbed the information.

"But that's exactly what I want him to do," Erin said. "I want him working the case, not sitting here playing video games with Jack or rocking on the porch with me." She looked at them. "I never thought I'd hear myself say this but I'm actually glad Tony's a cop. I know he's doing everything he can to find her."

Tess grabbed her chest. "Did you hear that? The lass said she's happy he's a cop. Patrick, you're a witness. You heard the words pop out of her very own mouth."

Erin smiled, which is exactly what she knew her aunt wanted her to do. "Okay, I give up. I'm happy he's a cop. There, I've said it again. But don't you ever tell Tony."

"Watch how fast I hit speed dial," Tess threatened.

They chuckled and Erin welcomed the lightened atmosphere.

"He's a good lad," Tess said. "Busy as he is, he still calls four or five times every day."

"Six." Erin looked at them. "What?"

They laughed out loud at her.

Tess offered Erin a glass of tea.

Erin shook her head.

"Lass, if you don't drink this, Patrick's going to hold you while I pour it down your throat. You've barely put a thing in your mouth in days."

Erin recognized her aunt's stern, this-is-not-negotiable tone of voice but still refused.

"You're not the only one who is worried and scared," Tess scolded. "We all are, but we're going through this together. We're family and that's what families do. We need to be strong. We need to help one another. Don't you think those children watch every move we make? They don't miss a trick and we don't need to be scarin' them any more than they already are."

"Your aunt's right." Patrick glanced at Tess and threw up his hands in mock surrender. "Yes, I'm agreeing with you. Don't bother faking a heart attack because it isn't going to happen again." He looked at Erin. "Don't you think we should hustle the children inside for lunch? I'll put the bikes in the garage."

Erin finally had a task to do. Something to occupy her mind for more than a moment. A reason to put one foot in front of the other and move forward. She patted the old man's arm in gratitude as she passed him on her way to get the children.

Less than thirty minutes later, the five of them gathered around the kitchen table. Erin presented a platter of peanut butter and jelly sandwiches, potato chips, apple slices and juice for the kids.

"Yay, my favorite," Jack said, already mumbling with peanut butter stuck to the roof of his mouth.

Tess served the adults thick turkey sandwiches and coffee.

Erin examined the sandwich. Sour dough bread, lettuce, tomato, mayonnaise and, at least, two inches of meat.

"The woman knows the way to a man's heart, doesn't

she?" Patrick asked no one in particular. He attacked his lunch with gusto.

"Tess," Erin laughed. "You can't possibly think I'm going to eat all this. I can't even fit my mouth around it."

"Pretend you're mad," Tess said. "Your mouth opens pretty wide when you're yellin'."

Erin grinned, squeezed the bread together as tightly as she could and took a bite. The first bite managed to stay down despite her roiling stomach. The second bite she actually enjoyed. By the time she finished, she was grateful her aunt had been so insistent. It was delicious and she hadn't realized just how hungry she had been.

Jack's plate was already half-empty. Amy played with her food but didn't eat any of it. Erin slid closer to the child and picked up a sandwich triangle. "Here, Amy, take a bite of your sandwich."

Amy turned her head away.

"C'mon, honey. It's peanut butter and jelly." She held the sandwich toward the child's mouth.

Amy clamped her lips closed, pushed Erin's arm away and turned her head.

Erin picked up a small slice of apple. "How about taking a bite of apple?"

"No." Amy folded her little arms across her chest and ducked her head down so Erin couldn't reach her mouth.

Erin sighed. She had forgotten how stubborn the child could be.

"Eat, Amy. It's good," Jack said.

Amy looked at Jack and shook her head no.

"You'll be sorry." He picked up the last wedge, waved it back and forth in front of his face. "Mmm-mmm," he said, took a bite and smacked his lips.

Amy watched him.

Jack repeated his performance, peanut butter and jelly oozing out the corners of his mouth. "Yum." He took another bite.

Amy lifted her sandwich, took a bite and grinned.

The adults laughed and clapped.

"See," said Tess. "Adults don't know anything, but Jack can do no wrong in Amy's world."

"That's the way it should be," Patrick said. "Follow the male lead."

Tess lifted Patrick's empty plate. "And to think I was just about to sweeten your coffee with my famous Irish recipe. But not anymore. Put that in your pipe and smoke it."

Patrick laughed out loud.

Erin couldn't help but smile at the interaction between them. Their friendship with each other seemed to grow with each passing day. *Love blossoming at their age. Maybe there was hope for her yet.* Tony's face flashed into her mind.

Erin left her aunt to finish the dishes and she took the children to get washed and ready for their naps.

"Will you read us a story?" Jack asked.

Amy jumped up from her bed, grabbed a book, held it upside down and pretended to be reading.

"Jack, you know story time is for nighttime, not naps." Erin took the book from Amy's hands and tucked her back under the covers.

"I don't want to take a nap."

Erin sat on the edge of his bed. "Sure you do."

"I do?"

"Uh-huh, because only rested children get to stay up late tonight, eat popcorn and watch *The Little Mermaid*." Erin smoothed back his hair.

Jack squeezed his eyes tightly shut and pretended to snore.

"See you in a little while." Erin closed the bedroom door. She stopped in the bathroom, ran a comb through her hair and threw some water on her face before she headed back to the kitchen. She had just finished sweeping the floor when she heard Patrick call through the screen door.

"Tony's here."

Tony. Her heart leaped in her chest just at the mention of his name. She hadn't realized how much she'd missed seeing him these past few days. She put down the broom and hurried onto the porch. Standing beside Patrick and Tess, she watched him get out of his car. She drank in the sight of him. His thick, unkempt hair looked like he had raked his fingers through it a million times. Dark, masculine shades covered those beautiful brown eyes. His white shirtsleeves were rolled up to his elbows. His tie was loosened.

I guess it's true what Aunt Tess says about absence making the heart grow fonder. I've missed you, Tony. I want you in my life. She smiled. *Who knew?* Her smile widened. *Just everybody in the whole wide world except me.*

She watched him take off his sunglasses, tuck them in his shirt pocket and start walking across the lawn.

Erin raised a hand and shaded her eyes against the sun. He walked slowly, purposely and his shoulders sagged as if he carried the weight of the world.

The smile faded from her face.

He climbed the stairs and stood inches from her, not acknowledging Tess or Patrick.

"Erin…" His voice matched the anguish she saw in his eyes.

"No," she whispered, clutching her throat with her hand.

He gently touched her cheek. "I'm so sorry, Erin."

"No," she screamed. She pounded his chest again and again. "Noooooo."

He gathered her against him, supporting her collapsing weight with his body. He stroked her hair and whispered comforting words in her ear but her mind refused to hear.

Erin's stomach roiled and bile rose to the back of her throat. She lifted her head. "Tony," she whispered. "Please tell me she isn't…"

Pain registered in his eyes. She read his internal struggle as he searched for something to say. She heard Tess crying. Slowly, almost robotically, she turned her head and saw Patrick embracing the older woman. She looked back and gazed over Tony's shoulder. Everything started to spin. Earth, sky, clouds, grass tumbled together in unfocused chaos.

Tony's hold tightened.

Erin buried her face into the soft spot below his collarbone. Clinging to him. Burrowing into the strength of him. The only thing keeping her from drowning in this tidal wave of pain and grief was the safe harbor of Tony's arms.

TWELVE

Erin stared at the white floral arrangement that blanketed the casket in front of the altar. *Carol loved flowers.* She glanced around the church. The pews overflowed with mourners. Neighbors. Coworkers. Former patients. Friends. *Look, Carol. See how many people loved you? See how much you'll be missed?*

Tears slid down her face and dripped onto her black blouse. She swiped a hand across her cheek and stared at the liquid. *Tears? I've cried so much I didn't think I had a drop of liquid left.*

Tony, sitting on her left, reached inside his jacket, pulled out a clean white handkerchief and pressed it into her hand.

"Thank you," she whispered, sniffing into its softness, and then wadding it into a ball in her fist.

Patrick's arm rested across her aunt's shoulders. Erin smiled. Tess deserved love in her life. Somehow it seemed appropriate that God would gently remind us of the circle of love and loss all in the same place, at the same time. She turned her head and she noticed Robert Stone sitting across the aisle. His eyes were red and swollen, his gaze unfocused and vacant. Erin had difficulty containing her surprise. Amy had been his patient, but Erin hadn't expected to see Carol's death affect him so profoundly. She puzzled over it for a bit. Robert had a gentle nature. He was probably thinking about Amy and wondering what would happen to her now. Still…

The service ended. Tony's hand on her elbow urged her to stand. Slowly, everyone filed out behind the casket. Erin squinted against the brightness as she stepped from the darkened church into the sunlight.

It's the kind of day you like, Carol. Blue sky. Sunny. Not too hot. I know you ordered this weather. I would have ordered pouring rain and pounding thunder. The heavens should cry just as hard as the rest of us.

Tony ushered her to his car. Once she was inside, he opened the back door for Patrick and Tess and then ran around to the driver's seat. A motorcycle cop, lights flashing, led the procession. Tony pulled directly behind the hearse. The short drive to the cemetery passed in silence, each person lost in his/her own thoughts and prayers. Erin glanced over her shoulder and out the rear window. Cars stretched as far as the eye could see. Again, tears welled in her eyes. So many people coming to pay their respects.

Tony parked the car, offered his arm and led her to a folding chair under a canopy. Patrick and Tess followed.

I'm placing one foot in front of the other. I'm sitting calmly with my hands in my lap. I didn't know our bodies came equipped with automatic pilot. Or is that you, Carol? Are you pushing me, pulling me, making me do everything right so I don't ruin your big send-off?

The minister stood at the head of the grave and waited for everyone to gather.

Erin couldn't believe this was happening. She stared straight ahead, unable to wrap her mind around it. Her best friend, her soul sister, was inside that ornately etched casket. She'd never see her again. Never be able to string popcorn or sit together and talk. Never laugh with her over the children's antics. Never *be* with her again. A sob clenched her throat, stealing her breath.

Don't worry about Amy, Carol. I'll take good care of her. I promise.

The funeral director handed Erin a red carnation to place on the casket after the ceremony. *You're not truly gone, Carol. You'll always be with me. Inside my memories. Inside my heart. And inside that precious little girl you've left in my care. Every time she smiles at me, I'll see a part of you. The best part of you. I'll see your heart.*

The minister looked over at Erin for permission to start. She nodded. He cleared his throat, opened his Bible and began to pray, "The Lord is my shepherd, I shall not want…"

Holding the binoculars to his face, the man watched the proceedings. After a few minutes, boredom made him lower them. It wasn't any fun watching from all the way over here. He wanted to be at the gravesite but couldn't take the chance. On television, the police expect the killer to show up. They pretend to be mourners, watch the crowd and try to identify "a person of interest." He was too smart for their tricks.

He thought about Carol. He had kept her alive longer than the others. She had needed extra punishment. Everybody thought she was so sweet and nice. But he knew better. She could be mean. Very, very mean. He made her sorry for the way she acted in the hospital cafeteria. He made her sorry for everything.

He giggled. Carol had been so excited about her date that night. She'd been so preoccupied with checking her makeup for the millionth time in a silly little hand mirror that she hadn't heard him approach. She looked surprised to see him when he stepped out of the shadows. The memory of her expression made him giggle. She was mad that he had startled her. Then, she got scared. Real scared. His giggles became a laugh.

He lifted the binoculars, focused in tighter and stared at Erin. More giggles escaped his lips. In a childlike chant, he sang, "It's your turn. It's your turn. Come out and play with me."

"I'm sorry about Carol. We'll miss her." The hospital administrator and his wife paused by the front door and offered their condolences.

"Thank you. And thank you both for coming." Erin ushered them through the open doorway.

Small groups of people still lingered around the food-laden dining room table and others wandered in and out of the house. Many of them Erin had barely recognized. She tried to be a gracious hostess but found herself wondering if they came to pay their respects or if the notoriety of Carol's death brought them out to gawk and gossip. She nodded and politely smiled whenever someone caught her eye, but she avoided conversation while she walked through the rooms and down the hall to check on the children.

Erin eased open the bedroom door and stepped inside. Jack had kicked off his blanket. Bending down, she picked it up, tucked it back around him and kissed his forehead. Stepping across to the other twin bed, Erin stared down at Amy. The child's thumb rested loosely between her partially opened lips. Her flushed cheeks resembled an artist's rendition of a cherub, her chest rose and fell in the natural rhythm of sleep. Tears welled in Erin's eyes but she held them back.

"Are you okay?"

Erin started at the sound of the male voice and looked up to see Tony standing in the doorway. She placed a silencing finger against her lips and gestured him out of the room, pulling the door closed behind her.

"I'm fine," she whispered. "Let's talk someplace else. I don't want to wake them."

He clasped her hand, weaved through the small crowd of people in the kitchen and didn't stop until they reached the steps on the back deck. He sat on the top step and pulled her down beside him.

"I can't sit out here," Erin protested. "I have to help Tess. There are still people in the house. Did you see the food? I've never seen so many casseroles in my life. We couldn't possibly eat all that food. I have to help her pack it up and—"

"Tess is in her glory." He cradled her against his side. "She's doing what she does best and what makes her feel the most useful. She doesn't need you in there right now."

Erin contemplated his words. He was right. They were all coping with their grief in their own way. Tess needed to feel useful and to stay busy.

Tony tilted her chin and smiled into her eyes. "Besides, last time I looked, Patrick was wrapped in an apron and drying dishes. I don't think we should ruin a beautiful thing."

Erin returned the smile and nodded.

"You look exhausted." Tony brushed a lock of hair from her forehead.

"I am exhausted. I don't think I've had more than four hours of solid sleep at one time since Carol disappeared." She gently eased away from him, not wanting to be comforted or to feel that all was right with the world when it wasn't. Instead of taking offense, he seemed to understand and remained beside her in companionable silence.

"I can't believe Carol's parents didn't come. What kind of people don't come to their only daughter's funeral?"

"The kind of parents who are scared to death they may be asked to care for their Down syndrome grandchild." Erin couldn't stop her teeth from clenching or keep anger from lacing her words.

"Have they ever met Amy?" Tony asked.

"No. They couldn't understand her insistence to have a child without a man in her life. Her father is a minister of an ultraconservative church. He believes anything other than conceiving through marriage is a sin."

Tony shook his head but refrained from comment.

"Did Carol know about Amy before she was born?"

"Yes. But she loved Amy from the very first ultrasound." Erin swiped a tear off her cheek. "And once she actually held her…no one could pry that child away."

Tony smiled. "I can understand why. She's a beautiful little girl. And what a personality."

Erin smiled. "I couldn't agree more."

"And the grandparents? They didn't come around after Amy was born?"

"When Carol discovered she carried a Down syndrome baby, her parents took it as a sign God was punishing her. They disowned her. They haven't spoken since."

"Remind me not to visit their church. Seems the preacher missed the lessons the Bible teaches on forgiveness and compassion."

Erin nodded.

"What happens to Amy now?"

"I adopt her."

Tony raised an eyebrow. "Can you do that? I mean, legally?"

"After my father died, Carol and I became sensitive to our situations as single mothers and wanted to protect our children. We had a lawyer draw up guardian papers years ago. She'd raise Jack if anything happened to me and I'd raise Amy if…" Erin's body shuddered. "It was a safety precaution like air bags in automobiles. You never expect them to go off, but you feel safer knowing they're in place."

Tony squeezed her hand.

"I'm having such a hard time believing Carol's gone. I don't know if I'll ever be able to accept it. We've been friends our entire lives. She helped me through my divorce. And I was there for her through her pregnancy. She helped me find my faith. How do you say goodbye to the other half of your heart?"

Erin silently stared at a dark cloud hugging the horizon and watched the sun begin to slip behind it. "Who was she dating, Tony?" She turned and looked him straight in the eyes. "I want to know. Who was the man that reported Carol missing?"

Tony clasped his hands together, holding them in front of him. "Erin, we've been over this a million times. I can't tell you his name. It's part of an ongoing investigation."

"I don't care about your investigation. Tell me. I need to know his name." She couldn't keep the rage and grief out of her voice.

"Please, Erin, I can't."

"You mean you won't." She jumped up and stormed across the yard.

"Wait!" He caught up with her, grabbed her arm and spun her to face him. "What good would it do if I did?"

"Maybe I know him. Maybe I can talk to him. Maybe he'll tell me things he won't tell the police. Not everybody likes to spill their guts to men in blue, you know." She hugged her arms tightly across her chest, not sure whether she was holding in the pain or trying to keep it out.

"Even if I could tell you, I wouldn't. Do you think I want you questioning potential suspects?" He ran his hand over his head. "Don't you get it? You're in danger. You fit the profile of the women being killed. The anonymous phone calls. The dead rose and poem. A single mom of a handicapped kid." The anger and frustration in his voice rose with every word. "And you want to go out and stir things up by playing cop? What's the matter with you? Why don't you just paint a huge target on your back?"

"Well, somebody has to do something. It's obvious you're not getting anywhere."

An angry flush tinged his skin. His lips thinned into a grim slash across his face. "That's not fair."

Deep inside she knew he was right. She was being terribly unfair, but she couldn't seem to stop. "Maybe this Mystery Man you're protecting killed her."

"I don't think so."

"*You* don't think so? You! Mr. Macho Cop. Mr. Know-It-All. How do you know he isn't the one? How? And if he isn't, then who is?"

"I don't know. Okay?" he yelled back. "Are you happy now? I don't have a clue and it's killing me to feel so powerless."

They glared at each other, hands on hips, chests heaving with the exertion of their argument. Tony recovered first. He clenched his fists at his sides and took several deep breaths. When he looked up, his eyes held compassion. His voice rang steady and calm. "If I could bring her back, Erin, I would. But I can't." His gaze locked with hers. "The only thing I can do now is find her killer." He stepped closer. "I'm so sorry. I tried to find her in time. I did everything humanly possible to bring her home."

Tears spilled from Erin's eyes and flowed like a twisting river down her cheeks. "I know," she whispered. And she did know it. He had worked day and night to try and find Carol. So why was she lashing out at the one person who brought her the most comfort?

"I promise you, I'm fully investigating this man," Tony said. "Just because I don't think he did it, doesn't mean I'm not turning over every rock and stone to prove it one way or the other."

She nodded and hung her head.

"You need to trust me. Let me do my job." Tony clasped her hand and led her back to the porch steps. When she was seated, he stared down at her. "Meanwhile, you need to continue to keep your guard up. Keep your doors and windows locked. Don't go anywhere alone. And call me immediately if anything out of the ordinary happens. I don't care how inconsequential you think it is."

"Do you think Jack and Tess are in danger?" She could barely put the terrifying thought into words.

"No." He traced his fingers across her cheek. "So far, it appears he's only interested in the mothers."

"Lucky me."

Tony's cell phone rang. He answered it, mumbled a word or two and slid it back into his pocket. "I have to go." He pressed his lips against her forehead. "Try and get some rest. I'll stop by tomorrow."

She patted his hand resting on her shoulder, smiled and said, "Stay safe." No sooner had the words escaped her lips then a feeling of déjà vu washed over her. She used to speak those words every night to her father as he left for work. History repeating itself. A shudder raced down her spine.

Erin remained on the porch steps after he left. The clouds on the horizon darkened and multiplied. The underside of the leaves danced in the breeze. A low, distant rumbling of thunder filled the air.

Finally, here comes the rain.

THIRTEEN

Three days later

The door slammed against the wall. "Mommy, I want you to send Amy home right now."

Erin glanced up from making Jack's bed. "You know you don't mean that." Erin skirted around his walker and straightened the spread on the other side of the bed.

"Yes, I do." Jack lumbered to the closet and tried to drag out a small suitcase. "I'll help you pack."

Erin took the case out of his hand and put it back in the closet. "What's got into you? Amy's your best friend. This isn't the way we treat our friends." She returned to making the bed.

"She broke off Luke Skywalker's arm." His lower lip jutted out in a pout.

"I'm sure it was an accident. Bring him to me. Maybe I can fix him." Erin fluffed the pillow and tucked the spread beneath it.

"She knocked down my Lego village. Now, it's ruined."

Erin stopped what she was doing and took a hard look at her son. His flushed cheeks and rapid blinking revealed how hard he tried not to cry. Something was wrong. Something much more than a few broken toys.

Erin perched on the edge of the bed. "I'm sorry, honey. That's my fault. I should have kept Amy with me while I cleaned. But you're a wonderful builder. I bet you can build a bigger and even better village. I promise I won't let her near it this time." Erin patted the spread for him to sit beside her, but he ignored the gesture.

"She ate my oatmeal and raisin cookie. I hid it in my Spider-Man lunch box. She found it and ate it."

Erin hid her smile. "I'll tell you what. As soon as I run the vacuum in here, the three of us will make a whole batch of oatmeal and raisin cookies. How's that sound?"

"No!" Jack's eyes glistened with tears. "I want her to go home right now."

Erin gently pushed his walker to the side and lifted her son to sit beside her. "I thought you liked having Amy here."

Jack hung his head. "I don't. I want her mommy to come back."

Erin drew in a sharp breath. She paused for a moment and considered her words. "I want that, too, honey. But Amy's mommy is in heaven. She isn't coming back. We're her family now."

"Did Amy's mommy want to go away? Didn't she love Amy?"

"Oh, Jack, don't ever think that. Amy's mommy loved her very, very much."

"Then why did she go away and leave her with us?"

Erin put her arm around her son's shoulders. "I told you, sweetheart. A very bad man hurt Amy's mommy. The doctors couldn't make her better. So she went to heaven where she doesn't have to hurt anymore."

Jack's shoulders sagged and he started to cry.

"Sweetheart, what's the matter?" She smoothed his hair with her hand. "Talk to me."

"Are you going to go away like Amy's mommy?"

"What?" She tilted his face to look at her. "I'm not going anywhere, Jack. Why would you think something like that?"

"I heard Mr. Fitzgerald tell Aunt Tess that he's staying on our porch every night until the police catch the bad man. Is the bad man coming here? Is he going to take you away, too?"

Erin drew in a sharp breath. She was speechless.

Heavenly Father, what a selfish fool I've been. So wrapped up in my own pain I haven't paid attention to the pain and fear of the people around me. Please guide my words and help me comfort my son.

Erin blinked hard and searched for the right words. "Honey, the police are working very hard to find the man who hurt Amy's mommy. They're going to find him soon, you'll see. I don't want you worrying about anything. No one is coming here. And no one is going to hurt me."

Jack's tears stopped, but his breath still held a little hitch. "Tony's a policeman. Is he helping to find the bad man?"

Erin folded her arms around her son. "Absolutely. Tony is searching for the bad man right this minute. All of his policeman friends are, too." She rested her chin on his head. "You know how good Tony is at hide-and-seek."

Jack looked up at her, thought about it a minute, then grinned. "Tony's great. He finds me every time."

"Yes, he does," she assured him. "And he's going to find this bad man. Until he does, Mommy and Aunt Tess will make sure everybody is safe. And Mr. Fitzgerald is going to help. And Tony is going to help. There's going to be so many people taking care of all of us that the bad man won't come near this house."

"You promise?"

"I promise, sweetheart." She made the letter *X* across her chest. "Cross my heart." She kissed his forehead. "Now, why don't we go into the kitchen and get started on those oatmeal and raisin cookies."

Later that evening, Erin leaned against the kitchen counter, a pencil poised above a piece of paper. "Pajamas," she called out in military fashion.

"Check," Jack said and Amy mumbled along.

Erin made a show of placing a check on the paper.

"Toothbrush."

"Check."

"Toothpaste."

"Check." Jack giggled.

"Amy's teddy bear."

Amy held up the bear and Erin checked the paper. "I must be forgetting something." She scratched her scalp with the eraser.

"Cookies," both children yelled.

Erin slapped both her cheeks. "How could I forget the cookies?" She slid a tin from beneath the counter and placed it in the overnight bag.

"Mommy, you teased us." Jack laughed.

"Time to go." Tess scooted the children toward the front door.

"Don't let them stay up too late," Erin said and followed them down the hall. "And don't let them eat all the cookies at one time."

Tess turned around, hands on hips, and said, "You'd think I never took care of the children before. What's the matter with you?"

"I know." She wondered if her voice sounded as sheepish as she felt. "But he's never been away overnight before."

"We're going to be right next door," Tess said.

"That's right, Mommy," Jack assured her. "Mr. Fitzgerald put up a tent in his living room and we're going to have an indoor campout."

Erin squatted down, eye-level with her son. "A tent, huh? That's pretty cool."

"And we're going to sing songs and play games and everything."

Erin tousled his hair.

Jack pulled back, his nose and lips twisting in annoyance. "Stop it, Mommy. That's what makes my hair stand up all the time."

"Excuse me. You're right. I won't do it anymore." One more sign of her little boy's growing independence.

When they reached the front door, Erin held it open and said, "I bet you're going to have the best time."

"Yep. And you know what? I'm going to let you use my spyglasses. Then you'll be able to look in the window and see everything we do."

Erin laughed. "You know, Jack, that's a great idea."

Patrick came up the porch steps and stopped in the doorway as Jack tried to barrel out. "Slow down, son. We've got plenty of time." He let the boy pass, stooped to pick up a package, and then handed it to Erin. "Here, somebody left this."

Erin glanced at the small brown package and tucked it under her arm. "I can't thank you enough for doing this for the children, Patrick."

"My pleasure. Now don't worry about a thing and go inside and get some rest." He turned and, whistling a tune, led the children off the porch and across the lawn toward his house.

Tess stood beside Erin and watched the miniature parade. "When you get to be my age, you can't afford to waste time.

I think after the children fall asleep, Fitz and I are going to have a long conversation about his intentions."

Erin's jaw dropped.

"What? I'm not getting any younger you know. All of this business with Carol—" Tess's voice faded away and a tear appeared at the edge of her eye. She took a deep breath, straightened her shoulders and faced Erin. "Life's short. I can't be wasting precious time." She hugged Erin. "And neither should you." She smiled and toddled off after the group. When she had gone a couple more feet, she glanced over her shoulder and said, "You know, lass, you're going to have the house to yourself tonight. You might think about arranging a couple of hours of police protection."

Erin laughed. "Don't worry about me. A certain detective should be stopping by any minute to check and see if I'm all right. Now shoo."

When the four of them disappeared into the house, Erin went back inside. Locking the door, she walked into the kitchen and placed the package on the counter before going to Jack's room to retrieve his spyglasses. She hurried back to the living room, knelt on the couch, held the binoculars to her eyes and laughed out loud. Jack, Amy and Tess sat in the window waiting for her. They laughed and waved the minute they saw her at the window. Erin blew kisses and waved back. The children scooted inside the tent. Erin waved one final time to her aunt, lowered the binoculars and headed to the kitchen.

She turned on the radio and listened to her favorite deejay, Samantha, field questions about relationship problems and play audience requests. The music temporarily eased her anxiety and created a pleasant, mellow atmosphere.

She lit several candles and distributed them throughout the house. She glanced around, satisfied that, at least on the surface, the house was back to normal. Her heart would take much longer to fix.

In the kitchen, Erin spent a few minutes putting cookie sheets away. She reached to turn off the kitchen light when the package on the counter caught her eye.

Curious, she slid onto a stool and examined it. Her name and address were printed in block letters on the front but there was no postage and no return address. It wasn't heavy. She lifted it to her ear. No ticking. She shook it lightly. No ominous rattling. She chuckled at her vivid imagination. She ripped off the plain brown wrapping. Placing the rectangular box on the counter, she studied it for another minute. No distinguishing marks. Just a plain white box.

Well, it's not going to open itself, silly.

Erin raised the lid and froze, unable to believe her eyes. She gingerly touched the green silk, thinking it had to be a figment of her imagination. It wasn't. Her missing scarf, the one she'd been wearing on the field trip to Disney, was no longer missing. Her stomach clenched. Her scarf, the same scarf Tony had said brought out the color of her eyes, was slashed in hundreds of pieces atop a note that read, *Can you feel my breath on your neck? I am Death and I am right behind you.*

Erin bolted backward, upsetting a kitchen stool. It hit the floor with a loud clatter and the sound echoed in the room. Her legs wobbled and almost refused to hold her upright. Someone had been close enough to steal her scarf yet go unnoticed. Close enough to place the package on her front porch. Here. At her home. Tonight. Her teeth chattered so hard her jaw ached. Tremors of fear shot through her body.

He's here. Outside my home. Hiding in the darkness. Watching me.

Unable to handle any more stress, she reacted rather than thought. She flung the box across the room and screamed.

"Erin!" Tony banged on the door and peered through the side window panel to see inside. "Erin, open the door." Adrenaline raced through his body. He pulled his elbow back, preparing to smash it through the glass, but paused when he saw a figure hurrying his way. He heard the dead bolt shift and he barreled through the door the second it opened.

"Tony," Erin threw herself into his arms, burrowing her face in his shirt, wrapping her arms around him. Her entire body trembled. "He was here," she said, her voice muffled by his shirt. She lifted her face to look at him. "The creep was here."

Tony eased her back, supporting her with his left arm, while retrieving his gun from its holster with his right. "Where?" He quickly scanned the hallway and the living room as he guided her to the nearest chair. "Is he still here?"

She shook her head.

He knelt down in front of her and lifted her chin. "It's going to be all right."

Clasping her hands in her lap to control the trembling, she nodded.

"Where are Tess and the children?"

"Next door with Patrick."

"Wait here. I'm going to take a quick look around."

"Tony…" She tried to grab his arm.

"I'll be right back."

He made his way through the house, checking closets, looking in corners and under beds, securing windows. In the kitchen, his gaze fell on a box on the floor against the wall. When he examined the contents, rage churned in his gut. He slipped his gun back into the holster and hurried back to the living room.

He found Erin kneeling on the sofa and peering into Patrick's house with binoculars. She spun around when she heard him approach. "The kids are fine." She placed the glasses on the table and sat down. "I'm so glad the children weren't here when I opened that package. I lost control. I would've scared them to death when I screamed."

"Them? What about me? I aged five years out there on the porch." He rubbed her hands, then perched a hip on the arm of the sofa. "Tell me what happened."

"Patrick found the package on the front porch and gave it to me. After the children left, I opened it and found my scarf and that terrible, disgusting note." Erin looked straight at him, her prior fear replaced with anger. "I don't want this maniac anywhere near my children. What can I do to help you catch him?"

Tony couldn't take his eyes off her. The flush of color in her cheeks, the flash of anger in her green eyes, the animation in her expression. He smiled. "You're beautiful when you're angry."

"Tony."

"I know." He raised his hand to ward off any verbal attack. "This is not the time or place. But remind me later to pick up this conversation when things have quieted down and returned to normal."

Her expression darkened. "Will anything ever be normal again?"

The sadness in her voice reached him at a level he had not experienced before. He wanted to draw her close and keep her safe in the shelter of his arms. The sincerity and depth of those feelings shook him to the core. She looked at him as a trusted friend. Nothing more. Nothing less. That's what he wanted, wasn't it? No strings, no expectations. So why did his heart skip every time he looked into her eyes?

"Why don't you go to your room and lie down?" he suggested.

"Lie down? Sleep is the last thing I want to do."

He tilted her chin with his finger. "Then don't sleep, just rest. I'm going to call this in and get some help out here. Meanwhile, I'll go next door to tell Patrick and Tess what happened."

"I'll tell them. I'd feel better if I could help."

He grabbed her arm and stopped her as she headed toward the door. "You can help…by taking some time to clear your head and get a second wind." He gave her a gentle push. "Now go. I'll fill you in on our progress afterward."

She moved down the hall, each step slow and cumbersome as if it took every ounce of strength she had in her body to keep moving forward. The smile slid from his face. He hit speed dial on his cell phone. "Hello, Spence? It's Tony. Listen…"

FOURTEEN

Erin opened her eyes. Light spilled in from under the bathroom door and illuminated her surroundings just enough to assure her she was safe and lying in her own bed. The digital numbers on the clock on her night table glowed 10:00 p.m. She rubbed her eyes, stretched and sat up. Two hours, gone. She could have sworn she wouldn't have been able to sleep. But then again, maybe sleep wasn't the right word. Maybe passed out cold would be a better description. Someone moved around on the other side of her bathroom door. Before she could be frightened, she heard a knock. The door swung open and Tony poked his head inside her room. "Good, you're up." He turned on the bedside lamp.

She shielded her eyes against the sudden brightness. "I'm awake, but I can't promise all my brain cells are up and running yet."

Tony smiled.

"How are the children?" she asked. "What's been happening for the past two hours? Have you…"

"Whoa." Tony held up his hand in a halting motion. "The kids are fine. Tess is fine. Patrick is fine. The house is fine. Everyone is A-okay and there's nothing to worry about."

"Nothing to worry about?" Erin laughed humorlessly. "A

deranged killer left a package on my front porch and you tell me there's nothing to worry about."

"Okay, let me amend that statement. No one but cops are around here at the moment. My team picked up the package to be checked for forensic evidence. The porch and the kitchen have been dusted for prints. Spence and Winters, the other detectives on the case, are in the kitchen waiting for me. I've called my sergeant and he's arranged for temporary police protection. Two officers will be here at all times starting first thing tomorrow morning."

"Tomorrow morning?"

Tony nodded. "Our bad guy has accomplished what he set out to do. He wanted to terrorize you and he did. You'll be safe tonight. I personally guarantee it. I'm going to be your bodyguard."

"You?"

Tony gently twisted one of her auburn curls around his finger. "Did you think after everything that's happened that I would leave you?" He leaned closer, so close she could feel a brush of air skim across her face when he spoke and could smell the cool crisp mint of mouthwash on his breath. "I'm not going to let anything happen to you. Trust me."

Erin saw determination and something else, something tender in his eyes. "I do trust you, Tony. I think I always have."

He pulled her into his embrace and gently kissed her. "I have a surprise for you," he whispered, his lips moving against hers.

Erin chuckled. "You do, do you?"

"Are you ready?" Encircling her from behind with his arms, his hands resting firmly on her forearms, he brushed her ear with his lips and whispered, "Close your eyes."

She did as requested and melted back against the solidness of his chest. Slowly, he urged her forward.

"Where are we going?" She hoped nowhere. At this moment she wanted nothing more than to spend forever cradled in his arms.

"We're almost there. A couple more steps." He led her across the room. "Okay," Tony said, letting go and stepping away. "You can look now."

Erin opened her eyes. She stood in the bathroom doorway and sighed with delight. Candles glowed from every surface, immersing the room in a soft, inviting light. A light floral scent filled the air. The bathtub brimmed with bubbles. A small stool, holding a tray of cheese, crackers, apple slices and grapes rested beside a crystal pitcher of iced tea on a small serving table he had set up beside the tub. Smooth jazz flowed softly from a portable CD player on the floor beside the stool.

"Tony, this is beautiful."

He stepped away and placed a towel on top of the closed toilet seat. He hung her robe on a hook by the linen closet. When he faced her, he looked embarrassed and unsure of himself. Maybe even a little vulnerable. "Anyway…"

"Anyway…" She gazed into his face. "I think you are the most thoughtful man I have ever met. Thank you."

The smile on his face reached up and lit the depths of his eyes. He was obviously happy he had pleased her. "You're welcome. I've got to get out to Spence and Winters. We've still got a lot of work to do. When we're done, I'm going to sack out on the sofa for tonight. Now get yourself into those bubbles before the water gets cold and I'll see you in the morning."

After he left, Erin undressed and slid into the steamy water. When was the last time she had pampered herself with a hot bubble bath? Eons ago. She leaned her head back against the tiled wall, the rounded edge of the tub fitting perfectly in the curve of her neck and basked in the water's warmth. The smooth jazz sound of saxophones wooed her with their melancholy. The floral scent and the room's candlelight glow added the final touch to an already-surreal experience.

Erin's eyes burned with unexpected tears. *You were right, Carol. Why didn't I listen to you? Tony is everything I could ever want in a man. I've been a fool about a lot of things lately. About time I got my head on straight, don't you think?* Erin wiped the tears on her cheeks with the back of her hand. *I wish you were still here. I wish I could tell you what he did for me tonight.* The candles flickered like a sudden wisp of air had passed by and a trace of a smile curved her lips. *Maybe you already know.* She took a sip of her iced tea. *I miss you, Carol. I always will.*

Erin lingered in the tub until the water turned ice-cold and gooseflesh covered her skin. She dried herself quickly and dressed in a T-shirt and jeans. She finger-combed her hair and applied a soft-colored lipstick. She couldn't do much about her puffy eyes, but she was determined to appear as calm and in control as possible. Taking a long look in the mirror, she approved of her appearance. If she could help it, no one would look at her and know that inside reigned chaos, fear and grief.

Erin knelt beside her bed and prayed. She expressed her gratitude that the children hadn't been home this evening. That Tony and his team were down the hall working into the wee hours of the night trying to catch this killer. She asked God to continue to protect her family and help her deal with the smothering weight of her grief.

Picking up the Bible from her nightstand, she decided to go see what was going on. She promised herself she would stay out of the way and wouldn't interfere. She could sit quietly in a corner and read. Or maybe she'd go next door and camp out in the living room with the kids. No matter what, she knew she couldn't stay here alone in the dark.

Erin moved on the pads of her feet as silently as a cat. She paused in the foyer. Every light was lit. Several police officers moved through the house, busy doing one task or another. She almost turned around and went back to her room when she heard someone call.

"Hey." In seconds, he was at her side. He tilted her face and studied her red-rimmed eyes. "Are you okay? The bath was supposed to make you feel better."

"I'm fine." She offered a weak smile. She was anything but fine. Moisture still clung to her eyelashes and her lower lip quivered as she fought back more tears.

He slid an arm around her shoulders and led her into the living room. They sat on the sofa and he cradled her against his side. He looked down at her. "Penny for your thoughts."

This time her smile was genuine and an unfamiliar tightness filled his chest. She looked so…vulnerable. He wanted to make all the bad things that had invaded her world disappear. No phone calls. No threatening notes or warped gifts. No grief or pain.

Erin gently clasped his fingers. "Thanks, Tony. For everything." Her touch sent a powerful surge of emotion through his body. He wanted to protect this woman at all costs. He imagined he would volunteer to don armor and slay dragons if it meant he could keep her and her family safe. He breathed in sharply and stood up to put a safe distance between them.

Safe distance? Who was he kidding? China wouldn't be far enough away.

The scent of spring flowers still clinging to her skin followed him. He inhaled deeply and tried to diffuse the escalating tension building between them.

Her body visibly shuddered. He didn't know if it was a chill after her bath or fear over what had happened this evening. He wanted to gather her in his arms and hold her close. But if he did, would she be able to feel the pounding of his heart? Would she sense that when she was near he couldn't draw a deep breath? Then he saw it in her eyes. Complete and total trust. After all, he was her friend, her confidant. Good guy Tony. He didn't need to be adding to her stress by letting her know how his feelings for her had changed. Particularly now.

Father, help me do the right thing. This woman needs my help, my friendship, nothing more. Maybe in another time and place I can let her know what she's come to mean to me...but I know, Lord, not this time and not this place.

His gaze fell to the Bible in her hands.

"What are you reading?" He rested a hip on the arm of the sofa.

She opened the book, removed a cloth bookmark and stared at the pages. "When the minister read the twenty-third psalm at Carol's grave, a certain verse kept pulling at me." She smoothed her hand over the page and then read, "'Yea, though I walk through the valley of the shadow of death, I will fear no evil for Thou art with me.'" When she looked up at him, her eyes shimmered with tears. "Do you think it's true, Tony? Do you think God was with Carol when she died?"

Tony slid to the floor and knelt on one knee so he could look directly in her eyes. "Didn't you tell me Carol had a strong faith?"

Erin nodded.

"Then she would have turned to God in her hour of need. I believe the instant she reached out in prayer He wrapped her in His presence. Evil may have claimed her body, but God held tight to her heart and to her soul."

Erin nodded and began to sob.

Tony continued to kneel in front of her and offered a silent prayer that God would help heal her broken heart.

When her crying slowed, Tony clasped her hands in his. "Give all the pain and fear to God, Erin. Let Him help you through this."

She lifted her head and looked at him. "I'm trying, Tony. But sometimes my prayers seem like mere whispers in the dark."

Tony smiled. "God hears whispers in the dark, Erin. It's His specialty."

Friday, 4 a.m.

You're letting him ruin everything.

He pressed his hands against his forehead. "Shut up!"

Stupid! Stupid! Stupid!

"No, I'm not. Leave me alone." He whimpered and rocked back and forth. The crushing pain in his head escalated. He squeezed his eyes closed as hard as he could. He couldn't think. He couldn't do anything with this pounding pain.

You should have taken her by now. You should have punished her for her sins.

A deep, animal wail sounded from the depths of his soul. He pounded both hands on the steering wheel. "Go away. Leave me alone."

Seconds passed. Minutes. The voices stopped. The pain eased. He could open his eyes. He could breathe.

He stared at the house, shrouded in darkness except for the light in the living room window. The cop was with her. A wave of rage washed over him. "No!" He slammed his fist against his thigh. He wouldn't let that cop ruin his plans. What were they doing in there? He knew. It wouldn't matter to either of them that other cops continued going in and out of the house like it had a swinging door.

"What kind of mother are you? You send the children next door because you're too selfish to be the mother you're supposed to be. Instead you invite him into your home, probably into your bed." His throat contracted with his screams. He choked and coughed until his eyes watered and his breath came in short, painful gasps.

He had a plan. There was nothing that cop could do to keep him away from her. Nothing.

He wiped the sweat from his forehead. A sticky residue clung to his skin. He lowered his hand and stared at it. Blood. On his hands. On the steering wheel. He stared at the body lying on the seat next to him. It hadn't been so messy with the women. Maybe because the man had foolishly tried to fight for his life.

He stared at the dead man. How ironic. A cop hiring a private eye. Wasn't that a laugh? The cop sure didn't get his money's worth. The private eye had been snoozing on the job. Never heard a thing until it was too late. He pushed the body to the floor and turned his attention back to the house.

Maybe he was wrong. Maybe Erin was upset about the gift he had given her and they were just talking. But he knew better. Erin was just like his mother, just like all unmarried women, selfish.

A tear flowed down his cheek.

FIFTEEN

"Do I smell bacon?" Erin slid onto a kitchen chair.

Tony glanced over his shoulder. "Good morning. You look wide awake and perky this morning."

Erin groaned. "I thought Christians weren't supposed to lie."

Tony chuckled and turned back to the stove. "Bacon and eggs coming up any second now. There are two aspirin to the right of your coffee mug. Just in case last night's tears left you with a headache."

Erin grabbed the coffee like a lifeline. "How can you be so cheerful after sleeping on that lumpy sofa all night?"

"Oh, I don't know," he said, emptying the contents of the frying pan onto her plate. "Since you didn't leave until four in the morning and the guys just left a few minutes ago, and it's only six-thirty now, maybe my body didn't have time to locate all the lumps."

Erin swallowed the aspirin. "Sorry. But wasn't that the best Bible study ever?" She grinned. "One thought led to another and the verses just jumped off the page."

Tony returned her grin. "The Holy Spirit blessed this house last night. That's for sure." He wiped his hands on a towel.

Tony busied himself tucking his walkie-talkie into the leather holder on his belt.

"Going someplace?" she asked.

"Sarge called my cell phone a little while ago." He turned to pick up his suit jacket. "The entire team has been called in for an emergency meeting."

Erin froze. "Did they catch him?"

"No, he would have told me if they had." He picked up his wallet and slid it into his back pants pocket. "But he seemed excited. We must be getting closer." He kissed her forehead and hurried into the foyer.

Erin followed on his heels. "Tony, wait." She caught up with him at the front door. "Promise me you'll call me the minute you know anything."

"I'll call." Tony stepped onto the porch. He glanced at his watch, looked up the street and then back at Erin.

"What?" she asked, joining him on the porch.

His expression showed every bit of his internal turmoil. "It's six-thirty. Last night, we arranged 24/7 protection for you, but the men aren't due here until seven. I don't want to leave you alone."

She laughed and grabbed the lapels of his jacket. She inhaled the musky scent of his cologne and fought the urge to bury her nose against the pulse in his throat. "I hate to be the one to tell you this, buddy, but it is not becoming when you act like macho man. Don't treat me like some helpless little flower who can't take care of herself for thirty minutes. I won't stand for it."

Tony grinned. "Ah, there's my Irish spitfire back again." He wrapped her in his arms and kissed her. He raised his head, but didn't release her. "Seriously, are you sure you're going to be okay if I take off?"

"I suppose you've never heard of dead bolt locks and pepper spray?"

He grinned again, released her and took another glance up the street.

"What?" Erin followed his gaze. "That's the second time you've looked up the street. What's going on?"

Tony wore a sheepish grin when he turned back to face her. "You're going to be mad at me."

Erin tilted her head and studied his face. "I'm going to be mad, huh? How mad? Don't-talk-to-you-for-an-hour mad or full-blown I'm-going-to-kill-you mad?"

"I've had a private detective watching you." The words burst from his lips, no-nonsense, direct and his body tensed, waiting for her reaction.

The color drained out of her face and her mouth fell open. "You've had someone spying on me?"

"No," Tony said. "I've had someone protecting you when I couldn't."

He stood there quietly and waited for her to process what he had just told her.

Erin could have sworn she heard Carol's voice whispering in her mind's ear. *Did you hear him, Erin? Protecting you. Because that's the kind of guy Tony is. The only kind of guy worth having…a guy who makes it his business to protect his own.*

Erin looked up the street. "Where is this private detective of yours?"

"Black car. End of the block on the right."

Erin squinted and stared into the distance. She saw the shadow of a man sitting in the driver's seat. She looked back at Tony. "He better not have binoculars in that car. The thought of a stranger staring into my house gives me the creeps."

"So you're not mad?"

She smiled. "No, I'm not mad. Actually, I think it was sweet of you. But if you don't get going, you won't have to worry about leaving me alone because the two policemen will be here already and you'll be late for your meeting."

He chuckled and pulled her close. "You're killing me here. Just when I'm sure I know what you'll do, you do something else. I can't ever figure you out." He pressed a hurried kiss against her lips, turned to go and turned back again. "Um. Tastes like eggs and bacon. I need just one more kiss to be sure."

Tony's lips banged hard against her mouth and his body jerked violently.

It took a moment for her mind to register what she heard. A firecracker? A car backfiring?

Tony spun around. He slammed his head against the porch railing, collapsing onto the floor.

"Tony?"

Precious seconds passed as she stared in shock at his unmoving body. *Tony?* She fell to her knees beside him. She touched the quickly spreading liquid that seeped from beneath his jacket in disbelief. Blood? This can't be happening. *Please, Lord, please, not Tony.* A second pool of blood began to puddle on the floor beneath the left side of his head.

"Stay with me," she screamed. "Do you hear me? Don't you dare die on me."

Her emergency room training kicked in. She pushed her emotions beneath the surface and assessed the situation, prioritizing her responses. She pushed his jacket open, pulled the walkie-talkie off his belt and pressed the transmit button. "Officer needs assistance. Officer down." She hurriedly relayed her address into the device and repeated it once more for clarity. She opened his jacket and quickly examined his chest. No exit wound. The bullet was still inside him.

She probed the back of his head. Her left hand came away soaked in blood and she realized his nasty head wound was the result of the porch railing and not a second bullet. The paleness of his skin and the fact that he hadn't made a sound nor moved a muscle since the incident made her stomach churn. She placed her trembling fingers against his carotid artery and felt for a pulse. Nothing. *C'mon, Tony. C'mon.* She pressed harder. There it was. Thready and weak but there. He needed help. Fast.

She grabbed the walkie-talkie, pressed transmit and screamed, "Officer down. Please respond. Officer down."

"Ms. O'Malley, come with me, please." Erin followed the detective down the hospital corridor to an unoccupied private room. He held open the door and motioned for her to precede him inside. "I'd prefer we wait in here if you don't mind. I've left word at the nurse's station where they can find us."

Erin took a seat in the recliner beside an empty bed.

Detective Winters extracted a pen and pad from his jacket pocket and leaned against the edge of the bed. "I know this is a difficult time. But if you could answer just a few more questions."

"My children?" Her voice sounded weary even to her own ears. The effort it took to raise her head and look at the man exhausted her. *Bone tired.* Now she understood what the term really meant. "Are you absolutely certain the children are okay?"

"Yes, ma'am. They're safe. Your aunt and your neighbor are caring for them in another part of the hospital. And, of course, my partner is with them until relief officers arrive."

Erin glanced at the wall clock. 11:00 a.m. *Take a deep breath. Relax. You know the drill. They'll come and tell you as soon as Tony is out of surgery. He's going to be all right. He has to be all right.*

The detective cleared his throat and poised his pen over his pad. "Ma'am?"

"Erin. Call me Erin." She shifted in her seat to face him. "Detective Winters, isn't it?"

"Yes, ma'am. We met briefly last night."

Erin nodded. "I remember." She pulled a thread on her jeans just to keep her hands from shaking. "I've told you and your partner everything I know. I wish I could be of more help but…" She shrugged. "It all happened so fast. I honestly didn't see a thing."

Winters ruffled through the pages of his small notepad. He cleared his throat again.

Erin's eyes narrowed. "What?"

"Ma'am, I'm trying to get an accurate picture of today's events."

Puzzled by the hostile tone of his voice, Erin nodded and waited.

"My understanding is that you've been receiving threats similar to the ones Carol Henderson got before she was killed."

Erin's stomach tightened at the mention of her best friend. She nodded again.

"Our unit arranged for police protection for you and your family to start at seven this morning."

"That's right."

"Exactly what is your relationship with Detective Marino?"

My relationship with Tony? After everything that has happened, I can't even answer that question for myself.

"Excuse me?" Erin squirmed beneath the man's penetrating scrutiny and stalled for time. She was a cop's kid. She knew the drill. Tony's not supposed to be personally involved with the people in a case he's investigating. This guy's wondering if Tony got too involved and that's the reason he was shot. Erin met the detective's eyes. "I met Detective Marino a little over a month ago. He's done a couple of favors for my family. Any other questions you have along these lines, you should ask Detective Marino."

Winters' eyes flashed. "Tony is a friend of mine, Ms. O'Malley."

Erin studied the man, his arms folded, his eyes smoldering with emotion. Anger? At her?

"I've known him for years," he continued. "If he believed a serial killer was a threat to you and your family, he wouldn't have left before the officers arrived."

Did he think she had something to do with Tony getting shot? Great. Like she didn't have enough on her plate without being a suspect in a cop shooting. Erin would have laughed at the absurdity of it all if she wasn't so angry. She bristled, wanting to verbally lash out at his censuring tone, but realized she'd probably react the same way if she were in his shoes.

"He didn't want to leave. But I assured him I was perfectly capable of taking care of myself for thirty minutes. I have dead bolt locks. Pepper spray. A telephone with 9-1-1 on speed dial." She hesitated before giving him information that might color Tony's professionalism but thought he could use it. "Besides, there was a private detective watching the house."

Winters impaled her with his eyes. "The same private detective we found dead on the floor of his car?"

His words hit her with the same force as if he had physically slapped her. "He's dead?" She squeezed her hands together to still their shaking. "But we both saw someone sitting in the driver's seat." *The killer had been in the car watching them. The killer shot Tony.*

"Detective Marino would not have put himself in a position to be ambushed," Winters said. "He would have done a visual surveillance of the area before ever stepping outside. He would have been alert, his gun hand free for action if needed."

Erin returned his gaze unflinchingly. "I told you what happened, Detective."

"If he was leaving like you said, ma'am, he would have been shot in the chest. So I have to ask myself, why was he caught off guard? Why did he turn around? Tell me, Ms. O'Malley, what exactly was Tony doing when he was shot in the back?"

SIXTEEN

The door banged open against the wall. Detective Spence entered the room. "Winters. C'mon. We've got to go." He stepped aside allowing Tess into the room. "She asked to come and stay with her niece. I didn't see any harm in it."

Tess rushed forward and threw her arms around Erin. "Are you all right?"

"I'm fine."

"We've got a police officer outside this door and another officer with Mr. Fitzpatrick and your children, Ms. O'Malley," Spence said. "You'll be safe here."

Winters rose from the bed. "I think Ms. O'Malley wanted to tell me something. Didn't you, ma'am?" Winters straightened to his full height and Erin understood how some suspects might feel intimidated during this detective's interrogations.

"No. I'm sorry, Detective. I have nothing to add to what I've already told you."

They stared at each other in silence.

"Winters, we've got to go." Spence's nervous energy filled the room. He fidgeted in the doorway, glanced down the hall, then back again. "Now, man."

Winters turned to leave.

"Detective Winters."

The man paused in the doorway.

"I'm glad Tony has such a good friend," Erin said.

Winters stared at her long and hard before replying. "Tony is a good cop and a decent man. It's easy to care about him. But something tells me you already know that, ma'am." With a brisk nod, the detective left the room.

"What was that about?" Tess asked.

"Oh, Tess..." Erin hugged her aunt.

The older woman hugged her back. "It's going to be all right. You know what they say about it always being darkest before the storm."

Tess and her sayings. Erin choked on a laugh. She needed this moment of normalcy. She needed to relinquish her feeble attempts to control a spiraling-out-of-control world and collapse in her aunt's arms where she could feel comfort and love. *No matter what happens to a person, life just keeps on going, doesn't it?*

"Are you sure you're all right, lass? I saw an ambulance pull up in front of our home. They wouldn't let me come anywhere near the place. For the longest time they wouldn't even tell me what had happened."

Erin looked into the worried woman's eyes. "That must have been very hard on you."

"Hard? I found myself standing right outside the pearly gates having a conversation with the Lord, Himself, I did. The way my heart was pumping I was sure he was calling me home."

"I'm so sorry."

"Nonsense, child. I thank God you're not hurt." She sat on the edge of the bed. "How's Tony? Have you heard anything yet?"

"No, not yet." Erin paced. "It's been hours. But I can't wait here any longer. I have to get to the children."

"I'm sure the children aren't missin' us."

Erin's pacing slowed. "Tess, I don't know how much more of this I can handle. I'm scared."

"I am, too. We wouldn't be normal if we weren't. There's a crazy person out there."

Erin nodded. "That monster walked up on our porch, steps away from our family." She heard the panic in her own voice but couldn't help herself. "He killed Carol." Tears burned hot in her eyes and streamed down her cheeks. "He sat outside our house…watching us…waiting…and he shot…." Erin choked on a sob. Stress cramped her stomach. She wrapped her arms around her waist to try and ease the pain. "I couldn't save him. I had my arms wrapped around him and I couldn't keep Tony safe."

"Stop it." Tess gently shook Erin's arms. "Right now. I know you're scared. You have reason to be. But don't fall apart on me now." She forced Erin to look at her. "There's no way you could have stopped what happened."

"Tess…you don't understand."

"I don't? I know you. You're thinking Tony was shot and you weren't. You're wondering why he didn't shoot you and you're feeling guilty about it all."

Erin's head pounded. She rubbed the skin beside her eyes to try to relieve some of the strain. "When did you get to be so smart?"

"At sixty-five I should know a thing or two by now." Tess took Erin's hand. "You think you're so different than everybody else? We all go about our daily lives like nothing bad is ever going to happen to us. But bad things happen to everybody. We all experience our fair share of troubles in this life." Tess chuckled without mirth. "Sometimes some of us even feel we get more than our share of those troubles…but evil…"

Tess shook her head side to side. "Evil is supposed to happen to somebody else."

Tess pinned Erin with her eyes. "An evil man killed Carol and shot Tony. You didn't cause it and you couldn't stop it. What you can do is not let it get the best of you."

"Just get on with life like nothing ever happened?" Erin couldn't mask the irritation in her voice.

"Of course not. How could we even try when terrible, horrible things are happenin' all around us? But are you going to lie down without a fight? Are you going to let that man scare you so bad you may as well have been shot, too?"

"No," Erin said with more determination than she felt.

"That's what I want to hear," Tess said. "You're a strong, capable woman. Face this head-on like you've always faced every setback in your life with courage and dignity. A little Irish spunk wouldn't hurt just about now either." Tess brushed the hair off Erin's forehead. "You want to feel sorry for yourself? Go ahead. Rant and rave for the next five minutes. You've earned it. But then you're going to pull yourself up and find that inner strength I've always admired. You're going to do whatever it takes to keep your family safe. And I'm going to be right here beside you helping every way I can."

Erin wrapped her arms around her aunt. "I love you, Tess."

"I love you, too, lass." Tess fished a tissue out of her pocket and wiped her own tears. "Look at the two of us. Blubbering our fool heads off."

The door opened and both women turned. A police officer poked his head inside, nodded to the two women, then opened the door wider and allowed a physician to enter the room.

"Dr. Patel," Erin said. "How's Tony?"

"The surgery went well. No complications. He's a lucky man. It could have been much worse. The bullet lodged in muscle tissue and didn't hit any vital organs. It was the knock on his head that concerned me. He was unconscious for a considerable time and it took more than thirty stitches to close the gash. Between the gunshot wound and his head wound, he lost a considerable amount of blood before he got to the hospital. But overall, he's doing well."

Tess threw her eyes heavenward. "Thank You, Lord."

"What about his arm, doctor?" Erin asked. "He's a right-handed cop. Will he be able…I mean, can he…"

"He's going to be sore for a few weeks. He'll probably need some physical therapy before he can fully return to work. But I see no reason he can't resume his normal duties with time."

"Can I see him?" Erin asked.

Dr. Patel nodded. "For a few minutes. He needs his rest. Because of the head injury, I've placed him in ICU overnight. He'll be sent to a regular room in the morning."

Tess patted Erin's hand. "You go. I'll tell Patrick the good news and tend to the children."

Erin followed the doctor to ICU. She nodded to the nurse sitting at the small desk outside the room and stepped inside. Her breath caught in her throat. She was a nurse. The sight of the heart monitor, IV bags and bandages shouldn't have fazed her, but they did. This wasn't one of her patients and nothing about this was routine. This was Tony. Her legs wobbled beneath her and threatened not to hold her up. She moved closer to the bed.

"Tony?" She leaned down and called his name again. No response. He was still under the effects of anesthesia. Erin checked the monitor. Blood pressure and EKG readings normal. A thick swath of bandages covered his forehead and wrapped around the back of his head. His skin was pale. She placed her hand gently on his chest. "Tony?" A solitary tear flowed down her cheek. "They say unconscious patients can still hear people when they talk to them."

She bent closer and whispered in his ear. "You can hear me, Tony, can't you?" She brushed her lips against his cheek. "You had me so scared. When I saw you lying on the porch in a pool of blood, I thought you were dead." She straightened and busied her fingers adjusting his sheet, moving his IV tubing. "And that's when I knew."

Several more tears joined her solitary one. She kissed his bandaged forehead. "I knew I couldn't take it if you died." She twisted wisps of hair on the top of his head with her fingers. "You see, Tony, I'm not as strong as everybody thinks I am. I don't take loss well. I know I would never be able to bear the loss of you. Because I love you, you crazy, wonderful Italian hunk. Isn't that a surprise?" Her chuckle ended on a sob. "The woman who swore she would never date a cop has fallen hopelessly in love with one."

Erin picked up his hand, pressed her lips against his skin. "But I can't do this." The sound of her voice was little more than a hoarse whisper to her ears. She cradled his hand. "I can't watch you walk out the door every day and wonder if you'll come home to me at night. I can't pretend not to listen for the phone when you're late. Or that I wouldn't be looking out the window every ten minutes for the police car that would bring me news of your death. Just like they did when my father died."

Gingerly she laced her fingers with his. "I didn't even kiss my dad goodbye. I was getting Jack ready for day care and running late. As he left, I yelled, 'Be safe.'" She chuckled humorlessly. "Be safe. Is a cop ever safe?

"That afternoon my father stopped a car for speeding. I often wonder what he was thinking when he walked up to the driver's door. Was he whistling, like he often did, figuring it was just another routine traffic stop? Was he cautious? Did he feel fear? All those years…and I never once asked him anything about his job."

She dabbed her nose with a wadded up tissue from her pocket. "I'm sure Dad didn't know a drug dealer sat waiting to shoot him to death."

Erin looked down. "Are you listening, Tony? Can you hear what I'm trying to tell you?"

Tony moaned. "Erin," he whispered so softly it seemed no more than a breath of air.

"Yes, sweetheart, it's Erin. You're out of surgery and the doctor says you're going to be just fine." She kissed the side of his face and rained kisses gently on his closed eyelids.

"I'm a coward, Tony. I don't have what it takes to be a supportive cop's wife. And I know that deep inside you know that, too." She laid her head gently on his shoulder and wept. Afternoon shadows fell in waves across the bed. She stood and looked down one more time at the sleeping man. Her lips curved into a smile that held no joy. "Goodbye, Tony." Without another word, she walked away.

He sat behind the wheel of his car and watched the entourage exit the hospital. He cursed aloud and then cursed again. He thought shooting that cop would have cleared his way. Now it was worse. More cops. They were like cockroaches. Kill one and a dozen more take its place.

He watched the family climb into a minivan. One cop got in the van with them. The other two got in a police car and he knew they would follow her home.

Go away. She doesn't need protection. She needs punishment. He laughed. Couldn't they see the irony of it all? They were

the stupid ones. She had them all fooled. The cops were protecting the bad guy.

He couldn't risk following them back to the house. He'd
already driven by once today thinking the house would be
empty, but he'd been wrong. Cops were everywhere.
Scraping. Bagging. Photographing. Like he'd be stupid
enough to leave anything for them to find.

"I'm not stupid," he screamed aloud. "I'm not." He
pounded his fist on the steering wheel. She made him so
angry. It had never been this hard before. His head pounded,
the pain behind his eyes intensified. He wouldn't give up. Not
now. Not ever. He'd make her pay. And he'd enjoy every
second of it.

He rubbed the space between his eyes and waited for the
pain to subside. *Think.* What could he do to get the cops to
go away? He rocked back and forth and moaned. *Think. Think.*
Slowly, he counted to ten. He took several deep breaths and
tried to quiet his thoughts.

When he opened his eyes, the solution flashed through his
mind and he smiled. Why didn't he think of it sooner? He
tossed it around for another minute or two and grinned. He
knew exactly what he had to do to get the cops to leave. He
turned the key in the ignition. *It won't be long now, Erin
O'Malley. Scurry away. Try to hide. None of it will matter.
Death is right behind you.*

SEVENTEEN

"Okay to come in?" Patrick ducked his head in the room. When Tony nodded, he crossed to the bed and made a show of examining the bandage on Tony's head. "Ouch, I bet that hurt."

"That's what you said yesterday. And the day before."

"Can't help it, son. Call it like I see it. Does it hurt?"

"Only when I smile." Tony smiled.

They both chuckled.

"How's Erin?" Tony, desperate for news, stared at the man.

"She's fine." Patrick pulled a chair closer to the hospital bed. "You need to start thinking about yourself, boy. You've got a lot of healing to do."

Tony waited until Patrick made himself comfortable. His eyes locked with the older man's and he asked again, "How's Erin?"

"She's safe. Tess and the children are safe. Your police buddies are with them 24/7. I can't be sure but I think some of them are showing up off the clock just to help out." Patrick chuckled. "At first Erin hated it but she's adjusted. She's actually making homemade cookies and hot coffee for each shift. I'll really worry about her when she makes doughnuts."

Tony laughed and then grimaced as the movement sent pain shooting through his back.

"What do they tell you about that bullet hole of yours? Are you going to be able to shoot straight after this?"

Tony admired the old man's honesty. He spoke his mind and didn't play games.

"I'll be fine. Doc says once the stitches are out I'll need physical therapy for a while, but in the long run, I'll be as good as new."

Patrick nodded, pleasure at the news evident on his face. "How much longer are they keeping you in here?"

"I expect to be discharged day after tomorrow." Tony shifted his weight, but it didn't do much to alleviate the discomfort from sitting too long on the mattress. "It won't be soon enough. I'm going crazy in here."

"I hear you. Do you need anything?"

Both men looked at each other and neither had to speak. There was only one thing Tony needed and Patrick couldn't provide it.

"It's been three days, Patrick."

"I know."

"Not a visit. Not a phone call. What's going on?"

Patrick shrugged. "If it's any consolation, she hasn't left the house. She keeps busy with the children, cleans, cooks and sleeps. The tension in the house is so thick you could cut it with a knife. We're all in some kind of holding pattern like an aircraft circling for a safe place to land." Patrick crossed his leg and rested his ankle against his opposite knee. "Sometimes pretending nothing is wrong is so stressful that I've considered trading places with you for a day or two."

"I have flashes, disjointed pictures in my mind," Tony said. Silence stretched between them. "I'm not sure if it really happened or if I imagined it. Erin was in my hospital room. She was stroking my hair and kissing my face…"

"I've had a couple of those dreams myself about Tess. Then I'd wake up."

Both men chuckled.

Tony looked away. The hollow, empty feeling in his gut told him it hadn't been his imagination. "She told me she loved me but that she was leaving me." Tony looked at the old man and couldn't keep the pain out of his voice. "Is that why I haven't seen or heard from her since I've been in here?"

Patrick squirmed. "Look, boy, I don't know what to tell you. Tess is madder than a hornet about the whole thing. The two of them are barely speaking to each other and I'm stuck right in the middle."

"So I didn't dream it." Tony laid his head back. "I knew it. I just didn't want to believe it."

Somewhere in the distance they heard a doctor paged. Muffled voices passed by their room. The oppressive silence inside the room caused the men to avoid eye contact with each other. When Tony spoke, he had a hard time keeping the anger and hurt out of his voice. "Nothing like hitting a man when he's down. I thought, if nothing more, we were friends."

Patrick ducked his head. "I don't know what to say. If it's any consolation, she looks worse for wear than you do."

"What did she tell Tess?"

Patrick shrugged. "Some mumbo jumbo about being honest with you from the beginning, telling you she didn't want to get involved with anyone, particularly a cop."

Tony squeezed his eyes shut. How could he blame her? Look at him. Shot and lying in a hospital bed. One of the reasons he'd never pursued a serious relationship with anyone. And the very thing that scared Erin the most. Besides, they'd agreed to be friends, nothing more. So why did he feel so cold and empty inside?

Patrick stood by the bed. "Give her some time, son. She's had a lot happen. She's lost her best friend. You were shot on her front porch. Some psycho is stalking her." Patrick patted his arm. "She's running scared."

"You're a good friend. Thanks for the visits. I appreciate them more than you know."

Patrick's voice sounded gruff. "Heck, I look forward to the visits. Being cooped up with two feuding women ain't no picnic."

Before Tony could respond, the door opened and Detectives Winters and Spence stepped inside.

"Tony." Winters nodded in his direction. "Could we speak to you alone for a minute?"

"It's time for me to head out, anyhow." The older man nodded. "I'll stop in again tomorrow."

After he left, Spence approached the bed. Grinning from ear to ear, he said, "We wanted to be the first to tell you."

"Tell me what?" Tony glanced from one to the other.

Winters smiled. "We've found our killer."

Erin peeled apples for a pie. "How much longer are you going to give me the silent treatment?"

"I'm doing no such thing." Tess, her back to Erin, kept washing the lunch dishes.

"You haven't spoken more than a half-dozen sentences to me for three days now."

"Harumph." Tess turned on the small television on the kitchen counter and pretended to be interested in the news.

"Tess, this is ridiculous."

The older woman spun around in a huff. "I agree with you on that one. This whole thing is the most ridiculous thing I've ever seen."

"Look, I know you don't want me to stop seeing Tony, but…"

"Whether you date him or not is your own business. But that lad has been very good to this family. He's done wonderful things for Jack. He worked himself half to death trying to find Carol when she disappeared. If you think it was easy for him to deliver the horrible news about her death, you better think again. He was like a rock for all of us through the whole tragic ordeal. He wouldn't have been standing on our porch in the first place if he wasn't there to protect you."

Erin drew in a deep breath and a sharp pain seized her chest. "I know. You're right. He's a wonderful guy. I've never met anyone as kind or considerate or dependable in my whole life."

"And this is how you say 'thank you'?" Two red spots of anger colored Tess's cheeks. "You leave him lying in a hospital bed all alone. It's not right."

Her own temper stirred. "You know I call the nurse's desk twice a day, every day, and check on him. And Patrick goes every day to visit."

Tess looked directly at her. "I'm not thinkin' 'tis Patrick's face the lad wants to see."

Erin allowed her temper to get the best of her. "Don't stand there and criticize me. You don't know how I feel. You have no idea how hard it's been for me." Her voice trembled and her hands shook. Ashamed for yelling at her aunt, she tried to rein in her temper. "I'm sorry. I shouldn't have raised my voice." She put down the half-pared apple and the knife. "Don't you understand? Sometimes the pain is so intense I can't even breathe. My heart is shattered into a thousand pieces and I don't think I'll ever be able to put it back together again. I love him, Tess. Leaving him was the hardest thing I've ever done."

Her aunt's eyes widened but she remained silent.

"Yes, you heard me. I love Tony," Erin whispered. "It's killing me not to go to the hospital to be with him. So maybe you could cut me a little slack here. I'm doing the best that I can."

Tess stared hard at her niece. "You're right. I don't understand." She reached out and squeezed Erin's hand. "But I want to. Talk to me."

Erin's eyes burned with unshed tears. "I've told you. I've told him. I've told everyone, but no one listens to me."

Tess raised an eyebrow.

"I've had such a hard time trusting men ever since Dennis walked out on us. I never wanted to give my heart to anyone again. Didn't believe I'd ever find a man worth taking that chance." Her eyes filled with tears. "And then I did. When I least expected it…when I didn't want it…there he was. Tony. Reliable. Dependable. Wonderful Tony."

She ducked her head. "And I could almost believe it could work out between us. But I know it can't. He's a cop. He's a man who carries a gun, lives in a world of bad guys and leaves the house with no promise that he'll come home at night. Every day I would live in fear I would lose him. The fear would become corrosive, eating away at who I am until I'm not me anymore. Until fear is all I feel." Tears rolled down Erin's face. "I love him too much to do that to him. To do that to Jack and Amy. To do that to me. I won't allow myself to become angry and bitter like my mother."

Tess recoiled as if Erin had slapped her. "Your mother?" She tightened her grip on Erin. "Nothing in this world could turn you into the shallow, selfish, self-centered woman who bore you."

Erin's mouth fell open. She had never heard her aunt say an unkind word about her mother.

"You think because I lived in Ireland that I didn't know what was going on here? I have tons of letters filled with my brother's torment. Lord knows he hadn't wanted to marry her in the first place." Tess sat down heavily, her legs no longer holding her up.

Erin sunk into the chair opposite Tess and stared at her in shock.

"I know I shouldn't be talkin' this way about the dead," Tess said. "But it's about time you knew the truth. Michael O'Malley was a good man, but young and sometimes foolish. He used to earn extra money doing odd security jobs. One night at some snooty high-brow affair he worked, he met your mother. She was beautiful and flirtatious and exciting…and drunk. He thought she was cute. He had no idea he was witnessing the tip of a major problem. He took her home and ended up staying the night. They had a brief affair, but Michael didn't love her. He planned to break it off, but she told him she was pregnant. So he did what Michael always did…the right thing."

Tess wiped a tear from the side of her eye. "He was miserable with your mother. She was a demanding, selfish and bitter alcoholic who made his life horrible. He worked two jobs, but the money he made was never enough for her. *He* was never enough. He thought about divorcing her a thousand times. But he never did."

"Because of me?" Erin asked.

"Partially. He loved you, Erin, with all his heart. Sometimes I think the only happiness my brother knew came from his time with you." Tess breathed in deeply. "Michael tried to make your mother happy. When he couldn't, he begged her to go with him for counseling. She refused. Michael learned the hard way that sin has consequences and sometimes those consequences can last a lifetime. Drawing closer to Jesus made him able to cope."

Erin cried openly. "I never knew."

"Well, you know now. I refuse to let you go on thinking all the pain you witnessed was because of your father's job. That's nonsense. Just like it is nonsense to think you could be anything like her. You couldn't even if you tried."

Erin straightened her shoulders. "It doesn't change the fact that my father's job caused his death."

"No, it doesn't." She stood and started to walk away.

"Aren't you going to tell me I shouldn't worry about Tony's job? That God is in control? Aren't you going to say I'd be crazy to walk away from the man of my dreams?"

Tess turned in the doorway. "Why should I, lass? You're doing a fine job on your own."

Tony stood at the hospital window and stared unseeingly outside. His mind raced with the information his team had given him. All he could think of was Erin. The news would be devastating and he wouldn't be there to help soften the blow. He was so lost in thought that he hadn't heard the door open.

"Hello?"

He spun around at the sound of her voice. "Erin." His heart plummeted to his feet. His emotions ran the gamut from elation to anger, pleasure to disappointment and pain. When had he fallen in love with her? Did he really think he could be with her every day, hold her in his arms and remain unaffected? Now look at him. Pathetic. Unsure of himself. The only thing certain was being without her caused him more pain than he had ever known.

She remained just inside the doorway. "I heard they're letting you out of here tomorrow."

"That's what they tell me."

"Good, I'm glad." She ducked her head and shuffled her feet.

Silence loomed between them.

"Look, Erin…"

"Don't." She raised her hand in a halting motion. "Don't say anything. Please. Just listen. I'm sorry." Her voice was a mere whisper and he strained to hear her. "I'm so sorry."

His mind leaped up and down for joy, but still he couldn't move. It wasn't pride cementing his feet to the floor. It was fear of doing the wrong thing, saying the wrong words and scaring her away.

"I should have been here with you. What I did was cowardly…and cruel." Her eyes seemed to plead with him for understanding. "Everybody thinks I'm this strong, level-headed woman who has total control over her life. But I'm a fraud. I don't have any control over anything and it scares me." She took a deep breath and then said, "When you were shot…"

She sniffed and struggled for control. Her green eyes pooled with tears and it was almost his undoing. Every bone in his body wanted to rush to her side, but he seemed frozen in place.

"I ran away from you because I couldn't bear the thought of losing you. But that's the irony of it all, isn't it? If I cut you out of my life, if I can't see you and hold you and talk with you, then I've already lost you." She took a step toward him. "It took me a while to think things through. Tess likes to say it's the stubborn Irish side of me. Maybe she's right." She shrugged. "But that's all I've been doing for the past five days. Thinking and praying."

He started to cross toward her, and again she raised her hand. "No, Tony. Please. There's so much more I need to say. And if you come any closer…" Her smile touched his heart. "I might not get it all out."

Patience. Don't blow it now. He waited.

Erin lowered her eyes. "My parents had an ongoing battle

they called a marriage. Their anger and hatred became as viable as a fourth person occupying our home. There'd be long stretches of ice-cold silence followed by bitter outbursts of rage.

"I always believed my father's job caused their unhappiness," she said. "Then when my husband divorced me after we found out about Jack's cerebral palsy, I didn't have a high regard for marriage to cops. Or, truthfully, marriage in general."

Erin shuddered at the memories and, suddenly, he understood how difficult it had been for her to have taken a chance with him at all.

"I was certain I would never allow myself to get into a relationship again...with anyone. It's just too hard." Erin looked up and her gaze locked with his.

Tony's stomach sunk to the floor like a lead ball. How could he blame her? Wasn't he a living example of her worst nightmare?

"I was wrong." Her eyes pooled with tears.

"Dennis left because he was shallow, irresponsible and selfish. And I lost my father to a drug dealer he pulled over for speeding. He had pulled over thousands of speeders in his twenty-nine years on the force. My father died because it was his time to die. People die every day. They die on the job, in accidents, from illness, old age. If I live my life afraid to love someone because they might die...or because they might leave...I'm going to live a lonely, empty life."

Erin twisted her hands, but otherwise, she stood straight, shoulders back, facing him with strength and courage.

"It took me time to come to grips with loss. And lots of prayer to try and sort out my feelings." She looked up at him, the tears gone. "I didn't want my marriage to fail. I didn't want to lose my father. I didn't want to lose Carol. But I did." She wrapped her arms around herself.

"I realize those pieces of my heart are gone and can never be replaced. But I also realize the only way to protect my heart from the pain of loss is to never love." Her smile filled the room like sunshine coming out from behind a dark cloud. "And to never love…is the worst kind of death. God knows how important it is to love. He made it one of His greatest commandments."

She looked vulnerable but determined. "I came here to tell you I'm sorry." She took a step. "I love you." She took another step. "And if you give me one more chance, I'll do it right this time."

The back of his throat burned with unshed tears and he swallowed hard to compose himself. "You had me at 'hello.'"

Erin stared at him for a moment, then laughed out loud at the reference to the *Jerry Maguire* "chick flick" they'd watched together after Amy's birthday party. She ran to him and he wrapped his left arm about her. He buried his face in her hair, reveling in its silkiness and deeply inhaling the sweet strawberry scent of her shampoo. *Thank You, Lord, from the bottom of my heart.* He lifted his face, gazed into her shimmering green eyes and his heart clenched.

Gingerly, she placed her head on his chest. "I'm sorry, Tony, for hurting you."

"Shh. Don't apologize. 'Love means never having to say you're sorry.'" The second reference, this time to *Love Story,* made them collapse against one another with laughter. He grimaced as pain shot through his body, but it was worth it.

His chin rested on the top of her head. He was happy. Truly happy. For the first time in his life. And he didn't want the moment to end. Selfishly, he cradled her against him for another minute, purposely closing out the rest of the world. Then, when he knew he couldn't put it off any longer, he leaned back and tilted her chin with his finger. "Erin, I need you to sit down. There's something I have to tell you and it's going to be hard for you to hear."

EIGHTEEN

Tony pulled over a straight-back chair with his left arm and straddled it in front of her. His expression made butterflies of anxiety dance in her stomach. The smile faded from her lips. She burrowed deeper into the recliner beside him as if she could escape bad news. "You look so serious. You're not going to take your turn breaking my heart now are you?"

Tony opened his mouth to speak, but before he could, they were interrupted.

"Housekeeping." The door swung wide and Jim Peters entered the room with his mop and pail. "Sorry for interrupting, folks. This will only take a minute." The janitor emptied the wastebaskets in both the bathroom and the bedroom. His quick movements and the furtive glances he tossed their way made it evident he didn't like disturbing them. True to his word, he mopped the room in record time. The man nodded and pushed the bucket out into the hall when Erin called to him.

"Mr. Peters, wait."

He turned in the doorway.

"I'd like to ask you something."

"Ma'am?" He had a hard time making eye contact with her. It was hard for Erin to believe this shy man was the same one who played so openly and naturally with the children. "I was wondering if you ever freelance outside of the hospital?"

A puzzled expression crossed his face. "Freelance? I've cleaned offices for some of the doctors, ma'am, but I don't do people's homes."

Erin laughed. "No, Mr. Peters. I'm sorry, I wasn't asking if you wanted to clean my house. I wanted to know if you'd be interested in doing your clown act for my son's birthday party."

He stared at her. "You want me to come to your house?"

"Yes." Erin's smile widened. "I watched you perform. The children love you."

He smiled. "Thank you, ma'am. I love the children."

"It shows." She crossed over to him. "My son turns six this Saturday. I know I'm giving you only a couple of days notice, but the children have been going through a difficult time lately. I hoped…"

He studied her for a moment before saying anything. "You're one of the nurses who work down in the emergency room. Wasn't there another nurse down there who got herself killed not too long ago?"

A wave of pain washed over her, but Erin kept her composure and merely nodded.

"I think I've seen the two of you around the hospital together. Wasn't she your friend?"

Erin shoved away her distaste for his questions. She knew it was normal to be curious, but the pain was still too raw. "Yes. Carol left behind a daughter named Amy who misses her mother. The child adores your clown act. I just thought if I throw a birthday party for my son and you perform, maybe it will help ease things back to normal a little."

"I've never done my act for anybody but the kids on the fourth floor," he said. "But if you really think it will help…"

Erin hugged the man and laughed aloud at the startled expression on his face. "Sorry," she said, taking a step back. "But you don't know what this means to me. I think a birthday party with a cake, balloons, friends and the greatest clown who ever lived is just the thing my family needs right now." She grabbed her purse, withdrew pen and paper and scribbled her address with directions to her house. "Here."

He read it. "What time do you need me?"

"I don't know. This is all spur of the moment." She thought for a minute. "How about two o'clock? Will that work for you?"

The man nodded and shoved the paper in his pocket. "I'll be there at two."

"Thank you, Mr. Peters." She watched him push his equipment into the hall. "Isn't that great?" Erin spun around. "Amy and Jack will be so happy."

"Yes, they will."

"You'll come, won't you? I know you need your rest and you won't have to stay long, but Jack would be so disappointed if you didn't make it."

"Of course, I'll come. Try keeping me away."

She smiled and hoped her love for him was evident in her eyes.

"Erin."

His sober demeanor worried her.

He stood up and cupped her hands in his. "They found Carol's killer. They arrested him a couple of hours ago."

"They found him?" *Oh, thank You, Lord. Carol did you hear that? They caught the creep.* "Are you sure? They really found him?"

Tony nodded.

"I thought you had bad news." Relief swept over her. "This is wonderful. The whole miserable nightmare is over." She wanted to dance with happiness. "I can't believe this. I have to go. I have to tell Tess. I don't want her to hear it on the news. You have no idea what this means to us. We were so scared."

He kissed her lightly on the forehead. "I know. So was I. But it's over. You're safe now."

"You know what this means, don't you?"

"Tell me."

"No more baking cookies or brewing coffee for cops." She laughed. "Except for one very special cop who is invited to be underfoot anytime he wants." She leaned her head lightly against the hollow of his throat, being careful not to put any pressure against the sling on his right arm. "If only we could have found him thirteen days earlier Carol would still be alive."

"I know." He held her closer.

"But I don't understand." She looked up. "Why did you hesitate telling me?"

A grim expression crossed his features. "Because you know him, Erin. It's a friend of yours."

Erin straightened. "A friend?" Her voice sounded incredulous even to her own ears. "No way. No one I know could be the monster who killed Carol."

Tony held her gaze almost as if he was trying to offer her his strength. "I'm sorry, Erin. Early this morning they arrested Dr. Robert Stone for the murders."

The strength drained out of her body and she plopped on the edge of the bed. "That's ridiculous. Robert couldn't kill anyone. You have the wrong man."

"I know how you must feel."

"You don't have a clue how I feel." Anger and disbelief laced her words. "You're crazy if you think Robert could do this."

"If it's any consolation, I didn't think he was capable of it either when I interviewed him."

Erin stiffened. "You interviewed Robert? When?"

"Robert Stone is Carol's Mystery Man. He's the one who reported her missing."

"I don't believe you. Carol would have told me if she was dating Robert."

Tony grasped her hand. "You were best friends. I get that. But even best friends have secrets."

"No. You're wrong." She pulled away from him and stood up. "She didn't tell me because there wasn't anything to tell. Robert was Amy's pediatrician, nothing more."

"Erin, think about it." Tony leaned back against the straight-back chair and looked at her. "You know Carol had met someone. You told me yourself that she seemed to be head over heels for the guy, but she wouldn't identify him."

"It wasn't Robert." Her voice shook and her words came out in a whisper. "She would have told me if it was Robert."

"Why? Because you dated him, too?"

"Yes. No." She looked at him in distress. "She would have told me because we were friends."

Tony tried again to clasp her hand. "If it's any consolation, she was going to tell you when she got home from her date."

Erin raised an eyebrow.

"Carol wanted to make sure the guy didn't still have feelings for you and believed that night would have cleared that up."

"How?"

"Stone showed me a diamond ring. He planned to propose that evening. The guy put on quite a show and I fell for it." Anger shone in Tony's eyes. "He sat in my office and pretended to be scared for her safety when he knew…"

Erin shook her head. None of this seemed possible. Her stomach roiled and she had to fight to keep from retching.

"How do you know it was Robert?" She swallowed hard to hold back the bile in her throat. "What evidence do you have?"

"It took us a while, but we finally made the connection between the women. Dr. Stone was their pediatrician. We almost didn't catch the threads because Cynthia Mayors switched pediatricians a few months before she was killed."

Erin pulled away and paced back and forth like a caged tiger. "So what if Robert was their pediatrician? Calling him a killer is a bit of a stretch, don't you think?"

"That's not all we have."

She waited for him to continue.

"This morning they found a locket embedded in the carpeting under the passenger side of his car. A locket with Amy's picture in it."

Erin squeezed her eyes closed. She knew that locket. It was a gold heart. She knew because she had given it to Carol.

"That's not enough." Erin wrapped her arms tightly across her chest. "All it proves is Carol was in Robert's car. If they were dating, then it's quite plausible she might have dropped it."

"You're right. There's more." Tony stood up and looked her straight in the eyes. "All four women recently changed their phone numbers to a private listing. Stone had a record of their new numbers."

Erin felt the blood drain out of her face and she feared she might faint.

Tony's grim expression told her this was as difficult for him as it was for her. She tried to keep her teeth from chattering as the reality of the situation impacted her.

"The locket wasn't the only item found in his car," Tony continued.

She steeled herself, knowing the worst was still to come.

"Several weeks ago we retrieved samples of blood and

hair from a piece of fabric found beneath Leigh Porter's body. We found a similar scrap of fabric in the trunk of Dr. Stone's car. We can't be certain until we send it away for DNA testing, but I'm expecting the blood on the swatch to match Leigh Porter's blood."

Erin raced for the bathroom and barely reached the toilet. She retched and then retched again, emptying the contents of her stomach.

Tony followed her to the bathroom. He wet a cloth with cold water and held it to her forehead. "I'm sorry. I wish it would have been anybody else."

Erin leaned back against the cold tile. Nothing made sense anymore. Her world was spinning out of control. She knew her shocked, disjointed emotions showed in her eyes, but she couldn't control her runaway feelings as she looked up at Tony, silently imploring him to make it all go away. "How do you date a serial killer and not know it?" she whimpered. "How do you care for someone? Become friends? Let them near your children?"

She covered her mouth with her hand and fought another retching episode. When her stomach settled, Tony helped her to her feet. She rinsed her mouth at the sink and patted cold water on her face before turning to face him. "How can I ever trust my judgment again? I brought a monster into my home and I didn't know it."

"Erin…"

"Robert was my friend. I cared about him." She laughed and the shrill sound hung in the air. "You're telling me that he killed my best friend." She looked directly into Tony's eyes. "And I was next."

Tony wrapped his unencumbered arm around her shoulder.

She clasped the front of his hospital gown. "I have to be

the one to tell Tess. She can't hear about this on the television." Erin fled the bathroom and picked up her purse.

Tony grabbed his shirt and pants from the closet. "I'm coming with you."

"Tony, you're not discharged until tomorrow."

"I'm coming." His tone of voice allowed no room for argument. He went into the bathroom to dress.

He signed the discharge-against-medical-advice forms at the nurse's station and ushered Erin into the elevator. Once outside, she looked up at him.

"Tell me this is a cruel joke. It can't be Robert, can it?"

NINETEEN

"Tony!" Jack pushed his walker across the floor with the speed of a winning sprinter in the Special Olympics and greeted the man in the doorway.

"Hi, champ." Tony ruffled the boy's hair. He tried to take another step when a thirty-five-pound force of nature slammed into his knees.

"Toe nee. Toe nee." He glanced down to see golden curls pressed against his leg and felt two tiny arms wrapped around him. He crouched down and hugged Amy, wincing when she bumped his right arm.

"Let Tony come inside," Erin instructed the children.

Tess placed a mug of coffee out for him. "You've been here day and night for two days now. You'd think you could run to the pharmacy without them actin' like they haven't seen you in weeks."

"Must be my charm," Tony grinned.

"Maybe it's the treats that keep popping out of your pockets," Erin teased.

Tony wished the smile on her face would reach her eyes. He saw her pain residing just beneath the surface.

"It's my birthday." Jack's voice spilled over with excitement. "We're having a party with balloons and cake and presents and everything."

"Cake. Ummm." Amy leaned her elbow on his thigh and grinned.

Tony laughed and then winced again from the sharp pain the movement caused.

"Tony knows all about the party," Erin assured them. "You guys better get out of your pajamas or the party just might have to start without you."

The morning passed quickly. They were still seated at the table trying unsuccessfully to explain to the children why apple pie was only a grown-up choice for breakfast and not on the children's menu when Patrick arrived. They set another place at the table.

Erin lifted Amy out of her booster seat and set her on the floor for the third time in the past hour, but not until Amy paid the toll of a kiss on Erin's cheek each time. Tony caught Erin's eyes and smiled at her across the table. *This* is what family is all about. Little things. Nothing things. Things he'd avoided and replaced with work. What a fool he'd been.

"Look at the time," Tess said. "It's eleven-thirty and I still have to pick up the cake."

"Don't get keyed up." Patrick stood. "You have plenty of time."

Tess chided, "Patrick Fitzgerald, I don't need you telling me I have plenty of time when I can see the hands whizzing by on that clock over there. Do you think I'm blind, old man?"

Jack and Amy giggled. Tony knew, like himself, they loved to see Tess and Patrick squabble.

"Oh, go on now." He waved his hand dismissively. "C'mon, old woman. I'll drive. Tick. Tick. You're wasting time."

Tess muttered under her breath, rolled her eyes and played the drama queen to the hilt.

Patrick chuckled and whispered in Tony's direction. "I love that woman." He lifted Amy into his arms and took Jack's hand. "We'll take the children with us. When we get back, I'll keep them at my house. You'll get more done without them underfoot."

Erin smiled. "You're a lifesaver, Patrick. Remember, the party starts at two." Amid a flurry of hugs, kisses and waves, she hustled the four of them outside.

Tony started to cross toward her when his phone vibrated. "Marino." He listened and then shook his head in disbelief. "I'll meet you at IHOP in twenty." He knew from the expression on Erin's face she was bracing herself for bad news. "Stone's out on bond."

Erin stood there, speechless.

Tony gently held her forearm. "Don't worry. Between the media coverage and our guys, he'll be under constant surveillance. He wouldn't chance coming anywhere near here."

Erin nodded but remained silent.

"I've got to go out for a little bit."

"I thought you were off the case?"

"I am. Officially, I'm on medical leave. But I'm meeting Spence and Winters at a restaurant. They're keeping me in the loop. Unofficially, of course." He planted a quick peck on her temple. "I'll be back in time for Jack's party. I promise." He winked and rushed out the door.

"We've got trouble," Spence said.

The waitress placed the men's meals on the table. When she left, Tony leaned his left forearm on the table. "What kind of trouble?"

"Alibi trouble." Winters swallowed a bite of his burger. "We checked and double-checked the time frames the medical examiner gave us for all four deaths. Stone couldn't prove his whereabouts at the time of the murders for any one of them."

"Yeah," Spence said. "The verbal time frame checked out. But the official written report that Stone's fancy lawyer dug up is another story."

Tony's insides tensed. He was grateful he hadn't ordered food.

"Originally, the M.E. gave us a four-day window for Cynthia Mayors's case based on the bruise discolorations she sustained during that time frame," Winters said.

"And the official report?" Tony asked, steeling himself for the information he didn't want to hear.

"In the official report, she extended the time frame three days. She stated the discoloration of some of the earlier bruising may have occurred over a seven-day period of time depending on environmental conditions prior to Mayors's death." Winters slid his half-eaten pancake platter away and downed a TUMS. "Best pancakes in town, but this case has my stomach tore up."

"So she extended the window to seven days," Tony said. "What's the problem?"

"During those additional three days, Stone gave a medical presentation in another state to several hundred of his peers." Spence waved his fork while he spoke. "We know it wouldn't bother the cold-hearted brute one iota to kill a girl on a Thursday and fly out and play Mr. Big Shot for a bunch of doctors on a Friday, but tell that to a jury. A shyster lawyer is going to push hard for reasonable doubt."

Tony frowned, stirred his coffee and considered what he had just heard. "The rest of the evidence is solid, right?"

"Yep," Spence insisted.

"What's bugging you, Tony?" Winters asked.

Tony shrugged. "I interviewed the guy right after he reported Carol missing. I didn't get the feeling he was involved."

"Yeah, that'll hold up in front of a jury," Spence said sarcastically. "Your, Honor, please drop the charges because I have a feeling the man's innocent."

Winters glowered at Spence. "A good cop trusts his instincts. But look who I'm talking to. You probably wouldn't know anything about instinct, would you?"

"I'll admit my instincts on this one could be skewed," Tony said.

Spence grinned. "You wouldn't be the only one. The FBI lady called it wrong, too. I've been waiting to point that out to her." He picked up his coffee cup. "I'd do it diplomatically, of course."

"Wrong, how?" Tony tried to remember the things Special Agent Davidson had said.

"She told us he was a loner. Disorganized. Labeled a creep. This guy is a media darling. He's on every upscale charity invite in town."

"When I spoke with Stone and, later, when I saw him at Carol's wake—" Tony shook his head. "I believe Stone loved Carol. I recognize grief when I see it. That wake tore him up."

Winters studied Tony for several minutes, then pushed his plate out of the way and took out his pad and pencil. "Okay, let's go over what we've got. Maybe we missed something."

Spence rolled his eyes, but pushed his plate aside and leaned forward. "Okay, one more time. All four victims were single mothers with handicapped children. Stone was their pediatrician. Each woman received calls that scared them enough to change to private numbers. But every number turned up in Stone's records."

Tony poured himself a second cup of coffee. "So the doctor has the new numbers. That's easily explained and certainly not ironclad evidence he did anything wrong."

"The nail in his coffin is the physical evidence found in his car." Winters poured a cup of coffee from the thermos on the table.

"Okay, let's look at that evidence," Tony said. "The locket doesn't prove anything. He dated Carol. She could have dropped it."

"And the bloody scrap of material found under the tire iron in his trunk?" Spence huffed. "That a date souvenir, too?"

"Let's play devil's advocate for a few minutes," Tony said. "Let's assume Stone is innocent."

Winters set down his cup and stared at Tony. "You think he was framed."

"Okay," Spence said. "I'll bite. Who had access to Stone's schedule, his files and his car? 'Cause if he's being framed, it's being done by somebody pretty close to him."

"What about the office staff? How many people work for him?" Tony asked.

Winters flipped another page in his notepad. "Two. A receptionist who handled the front desk and a nurse."

"Yeah, Pollyanna and Brunhilde," Spence said. "The receptionist is a kid fresh out of high school and the nurse has been with the doc since he hung his shingle out to dry."

"Besides," Winters added, "we checked them out. They're clean."

"There's got to be something we're missing." *Think. Think.* Tony tapped his spoon on the table. *Who else is a trusted regular in a doctor's office?* A prickly sensation crept up the back of his neck. Snatches of conversation and flashes of images raced through his mind. The janitor mopping the hospital floor. The same man who moonlighted cleaning offices but had never been asked to work outside the hospital as a clown. No. No. No. It couldn't be. "Winters, what's the name of his office cleaning service?" He held his breath while he waited for the answer.

Winters stared down at his tablet. "He doesn't have a service. He uses a private individual."

Tony's stomach clenched and cold fear twisted his insides so hard he couldn't move.

"The guy's worked for him for years. Works over at the hospital, too." Winters looked up from his pad. "The name is Peters. Jim Peters."

Tony bolted from the booth and dialed his cell phone before Winters finished uttering the man's last name. "Call for backup. The killer's heading for Erin's," he yelled over his shoulder and ran for the door. *Erin. Please, God, save Erin.*

The phone rang at the same time as the doorbell chimed. Erin frowned, decided the caller could call back, and hurried down the hall to the front door. She wasn't expecting anyone this early. The party didn't start for another two hours. She peeked through the curtains and unfastened the locks.

"Mr. Peters." Erin smiled at the man standing on her porch. "I'm sorry. Did I tell you the wrong time? The party's not supposed to start until two."

"No, ma'am. You told me two."

"I don't understand. You're early."

"Nobody's ever asked me to do my clown act in their home." He gestured with the small bag he carried. "So I thought I'd show up and help you get ready, ma'am. My way of saying thanks."

"That's so sweet," Erin said. "But everything's under

control. My aunt took the children to pick up the cake and everything else is pretty much ready."

Peters shifted his weight side to side. "There must be something I can do to help, ma'am. By the time I get home I'll just have to turn around and come back again."

"Of course, where are my manners?" Erin opened the door wide and gestured him inside. "I was just getting ready to blow up some balloons. Would you like to help?"

"I'd like that." Jim Peters stepped into the foyer.

Erin closed and dead-bolted the door. She felt his eyes boring into her back and it unnerved her. She turned her head and the intensity of his gaze caused a shiver to run up her spine. She shifted uncomfortably. Something felt off. Maybe this wasn't such a good idea after all. She opened her mouth, intending to call the whole thing off and ask him to leave, when the phone rang again. Both of them jumped at the sound. She hurried toward the phone, but the ringing stopped before she reached it. Feeling foolish for her uneasiness around the shy man, she mentally chastised herself. "Would you like a cup of coffee, Mr. Peters?" she called over her shoulder as she crossed the kitchen and reached up into the kitchen cabinet. She placed two mugs on the counter and turned. "Mr. Peters?"

TWENTY

The stealth of his movements set off an internal alarm. Fear slithered through her body. What was the matter with her? This was Mr. Peters, the clown from the hospital, the shy janitor, the man who graciously agreed to spend his Saturday afternoon entertaining her children. Why was her imagination running wild?

He placed his bag between them on the kitchen island and then he grinned. It wasn't a friendly grin. It was feral. Malicious. Her uneasiness escalated. Slowly, he eased his hand out of the bag. The reflective glint of metal drew her eye. *Oh, God, help me. He has a knife.*

"You fooled them," Peters said as he circled around the counter. "Everyone thinks you're Mother of the Year. Taking in another woman's handicapped child. But I know the truth. It isn't enough to ruin one child's life. You have to destroy two." His lips curled into a sneer. "You pretend to care about these children, but it's an act. I know the evil in your heart."

Erin's gaze flew around the kitchen, assessing both her situation and her closest means of escape. "I don't know what you're talking about."

The man laughed. "This is the part I love. Where the fly understands it just entered the spider's web." He sobered.

"Let me introduce myself. My name is Death and I am right in front of you."

Terror seized Erin's chest. She had to force every breath she took.

This is the day I die. This man killed Carol. He's going to kill me and no one will know who it was.

Panic overcame her and her body began to shake.

Help me, Jesus.

The twenty-third psalm popped into her mind. She began to silently pray. *"Yea, though I walk through the valley of the shadow of death, I will fear no evil for Thou art with me."*

The prayer grounded her. A wave of calmness swept over her and her trembling ceased. She knew no matter what was going to happen, she would not be alone. Staying calm gave her time to think. Her mind raced with possible scenarios that might get her out of this alive. "Mr. Peters…please… put down the knife." She kept her voice low and nonthreatening. "Sit down. Let's talk. Tell me what I've done to upset you."

"Do you think I'm stupid?" he roared, his arms flailing, his bag sliding across the kitchen island. "I'm not stupid."

She startled when he yelled. "No, of course not." Her voice softened to a whisper. "You need help, Mr. Peters. You're sick. Let me help—"

"Sick?" The singsong of his voice silenced her. "I'm not sick, Ms. O'Malley. I'm gifted. I can see inside people's hearts and it's my duty to punish the sinners." His voice lowered and the evil in his tone caused goose bumps to skitter along her flesh. "Your heart is the blackest of them all."

She coughed and hoped her upper body movements would distract him from her slow, side-step movements. "I don't understand," she said, bending at the waist, coughing, leaning heavily on the counter, then facing him again. *Eight steps. She'd made it eight steps closer to the back door.*

"I don't know what you think I've done." She moved another inch, then another. "I'm sorry if I offended you. Really, I am." She slid her foot three more inches to the left. "If you leave right now, I promise I won't say anything to anyone."

His sneer revealed uneven, yellow teeth, and for a moment, Erin pictured a vicious animal in front of her instead of a person. "Liar!" He pounded his fist on the counter.

The phone rang, startling them. Peters wailed and grabbed his head, rocking back and forth as though he were in un-bearable pain.

Erin took advantage of the moment and raced to the back door. Her hand closed around the door knob.

"No, no, Miss Erin." He taunted her like she was a misbe-having child. "You don't want me to shoot you, do you?"

Her mind raced. She'd only seen a knife. Did he grab a gun from his case? She twisted the knob even though she knew it was useless. He'd kill her before she could open the dead bolt.

The phone fell silent.

She reached for the dead bolt.

"Oh, goody. You're going to make me shoot." His voice sounded closer. "But I won't kill you. I'll do just enough damage to make you wish you were dead."

Erin had no doubt he meant every word.

"Killing comes later," he said. "Much later. First, you'll beg me to stop. Then, you'll beg me for mercy. Finally, you'll beg me to die."

Erin swung around, her body quivering with rage. "Is that what you did to Carol? Did you torture her? Make her beg for death?" Tears burned her eyes as she confronted the man standing only inches from her.

"You're quick. Figured that out all by yourself. Sit down," he commanded, pushing her into a nearby chair. He rubbed his forehead.

Erin tried desperately to stall for time as she searched her mind for anything that might help her find a way out of the situation. Maybe if she distracted him, it would buy her the precious moments she would need to get away.

"I've got some pain pills in the medicine cabinet," Erin said. "I'll get them for you. Maybe they'll help."

A flash of light, followed by intense pain, shot through the left side of her face. Blood pooled in her mouth. He had back-handed her with the gun. "You don't know anything about pain. Not yet."

Erin stared into the darkest eyes she had ever seen and knew she was looking into the gates of hell.

The phone rang again.

"I need to answer it," Erin pleaded, stalling for time. "People will worry if I don't answer."

"Shut up." His fingers dug painfully into her throat.

Erin clawed at his hand as she struggled to breathe.

The phone continued to ring.

"Stop that ringing!" With one angry yelp, Peters released Erin's throat long enough to pull the phone off the wall and fling it across the room.

The second he released her, she sprinted toward the hallway. He tackled her. Flesh ripped from her elbows and knees as she slid against the hardwood floor.

He yanked her around, straddling her legs. He punched her in the face with such force, she had to fight to remain conscious. Her jaw and teeth throbbed.

"Why?" she whispered, spittle and blood streaming from the corner of her mouth.

He placed his gun out of her reach and drew his knife from his belt. Without a word he pressed the blade against her throat, provided pressure and grinned. A thousand fingers of fire burned her flesh as he sliced her throat.

"Why?" He giggled uncontrollably. He took the tip of the knife and slid it down her shirt, slicing away the top button. "Before I'm finished with you, you'll know why."

He straightened, still pinning her to the ground with his weight. He lowered the knife. "We're going to get up now. You won't try to run, will you? Or the next slice across your throat will be much deeper."

"Don't move or I'll blow your brains all over this kitchen." Tony pressed the hard muzzle of his gun into the base of the man's skull. Relief flowed through Erin's body and her tears became tears of joy.

"Drop your weapon. Do it now!" Tony demanded.

Peters dropped the knife. He raised his hands in surrender and slowly started to stand. "I underestimated you, Detective. I thought you'd be out of commission after I shot you. Let's see, shall we?" Peters slammed an elbow backward into Tony's right shoulder. Tony doubled over in pain, his weapon falling to his side. In a split second, Peters launched his attack. He punched Tony repeatedly in the vicinity of the bullet wound. Tony fell to the floor writhing in agony.

With a shriek she didn't even recognize as her own, Erin jumped on Peters's back. Wrapping her legs around the man's waist, she desperately clawed at his face, gouging her fingers into his eyes. He screamed and tried to pull her hands away. Operating on pure adrenaline, she sank her teeth into the side of his neck. The taste of sweat and flesh nauseated her, but she held on to the bucking, screaming man as hard as she could. Peters wrenched her hair so hard that a hunk came loose in his hand. They toppled to the floor and both of them scrambled like crabs across the floor trying to reach his discarded gun.

Erin got there first. With every ounce of strength remaining, she rolled out of his reach. Jumping to her feet, she pointed the gun at the man's face. "Don't move."

Peters grinned and started to rise.

"Go ahead, you filthy piece of slime. Give me an excuse to pull this trigger." Tears of rage, mixed with blood, poured down her face. One of her eyes had swollen shut, so she had to tilt her head to keep him in constant sight.

"You wouldn't shoot me."

"Try me." She forced the words through a mouth so numb and swollen it felt like she'd had Novocain. Images filled her mind. Carol begging for her life, pleading to be able to return to her daughter. Newspaper pictures of three other women, lost to their families forever. Tony lying in a pool of blood. Amy crying and asking for her mother. Rage pulsed through her body. Her finger tightened on the trigger. She steadied the weapon with both hands.

"Don't," Tony whispered in her ear. He leaned heavily against her back as though it was difficult for him to support his own weight. His arm wrapped around her waist and his right hand slowly moved over hers. "Please, Erin. Give me the gun."

She couldn't let go. Her finger twitched against the trigger. She could easily kill this man and that self-knowledge scared her.

Help me, Lord. Help me remember judgment is Yours, not mine.

Erin stared at Peters. "Why? Make me understand."

"I did it for the children. Don't you see?" Pride shone in his eyes. "Now they have a chance to be adopted. To have a real family with two parents. They have a chance to be happy. I would have been happy if someone had adopted me, if I had had a dad."

Erin blinked in astonishment, her stomach churned. "What?" The shock of his words combined with this afternoon's trauma took its toll on her nervous system and her body trembled. "You killed these women because they were single parents?" She couldn't keep the incredulity out of her voice.

"Single moms of special needs kids," he spat out in anger. "Why do you keep us? You know you hate us. You can't do the things you want to do when you have us around all the time. Who wants to babysit 'special' kids? Nobody. So you lock us in closets with coloring books and a flashlight and tell us to be quiet. If we make noise, if we ask to get out of the closet because we have to go to the bathroom or because our flashlight doesn't work and it's dark and we're scared, you beat us."

He pounded his head with his fist. "You think we don't peek under the door and see you with all those men? You know how much we want a dad. So we sit in the closet. We wait and we hope. But the men don't stay. They throw money on the table and leave. You tell us it's our fault because nobody wants to be saddled with a handicapped kid. But that's not true. If there was a dad in the house, the kids would be happy. I need to give the kids a chance to be adopted. I need to give them a chance to find a dad."

Erin saw true pain in the man's eyes.

Peters lowered his head. His voice became a whisper. "Did you know most people don't close their curtains at night? I like to look inside. I see the dads playing with their kids. I see families eating dinner together. Everybody is happy. Nobody is locked in a closet." His eyes hardened when he looked up at her. "Kids deserve a chance to have a real family. Even a foster family would be better than a mother who hates you."

Erin tried to imagine what it must have been like for Peters. To be a child locked in a closet in the dark. Even though she still despised him for all he had done, she knew she couldn't hurt a child, no matter what the age. Slowly, she released her grip.

Tony grabbed the weapon and moved to her side. He held the gun in his left hand, his sling torn, his right arm hanging at his side. Perspiration coated his forehead. His eyes radiated pain. "Don't give me a reason, Peters, to pull this trigger. At this moment, it's the only thing I want to do."

"Go ahead. Kill me. Do it."

The front door banged open. Within seconds, the room filled with cops, weapons drawn. Winters hurried to Tony's side, holding a gun at ready, while Spence cuffed Peters and dragged him away.

Tony collapsed back against the wall, his legs barely holding him up.

Erin rushed to his side. Her fingers moved gently over his chest as she checked the extent of his injuries. "We need to get you to a hospital."

"Me? Have you looked at yourself lately?" Gently, he tilted her face. He grimaced at the sight of the angry discoloration on the whole left side of her face. Her eye was completely swollen shut. But he paled when he saw the red ribbon of blood seeping from her sliced throat. "Erin?"

Her hand flew to her throat. "I'm okay. It wasn't deep."

"You guys gonna make it?" Winters's expression made Erin realize how bad they looked.

"I guess I got your friend hurt again, didn't I?" Erin teased the detective.

"Naw," Winters replied. "From the looks of it, the two of you saved one another." He looked steadily from one to the other, and then nodded at Erin. "You did good, ma'am."

Erin tried to smile, but knew from the odd twisting sensation in her lips and the horrified expression on Winters's face that it didn't look much like a smile. Matter of fact, she was certain of it when Winters dashed to collect the gurney and the EMTs personally.

The excruciating pain in her jaw made talking difficult, but there were things she needed to say. "Thank you," she whispered to Tony through clenched teeth. "He would have killed me if you hadn't gotten here when you did."

His eyes glistened and his voice grew husky. "I was supposed to protect you. Instead, I left you alone which made you a prime target for a killer. Some job I did, huh?"

She cupped Tony's face. "You couldn't have known. No one knew."

"I'm the detective, remember? It's my job to know." Tony couldn't hold back anymore and his tears flowed freely. "When I think how close I came to losing you." He swiped a hand across his face. "I prayed, Erin. I prayed a million times on the way over here that God would protect you and help me get to you in time."

Erin curled against Tony's uninjured side. "God answered your prayers, Tony…and mine." She sighed. "I can't believe we made it through this. It's been a living nightmare."

Tony nodded, drew her close and rested his chin on top of her head. "I've been thanking the good Lord from the bottom of my heart." He kissed the top of her hair. "It's over now. You won't need me to protect you anymore."

Erin raised her face so she could look into his eyes. She

saw the doubt, the wondering if there would be a place for him in her life now that the crisis had passed. "I will always need you, Tony Marino, to love and protect my heart."

Their lips barely touched in the softest of kisses. But it was the kind of kiss that did all the talking for them, a kiss filled with hope and love and forever after.

* * * * *

Dear Reader,

Authors are frequently asked where they get their ideas. My son, David, is responsible for the birth of this one. After the unexpected loss of my husband, I found myself having a difficult time transitioning to my life without him. In an attempt to lift my spirits, he encouraged me to get back to writing. I had a partial manuscript aimed at sweet romance and another manuscript started about a serial killer aimed at romantic suspense. However, I had had a major case of writer's block for a long time and was unable to finish either manuscript.

My son suggested I combine the two. I said, "You can't combine a sweet romance with an edgy, dark suspense." He asked, "Why not?"

Why not, indeed?

The wheels started turning. People know bad things happen to everyone—but evil is supposed to happen to somebody else. What if evil moved into small-town America, stalked a single mom, raising her handicapped child, and brought terror and loss right to her doorstep? And what if this single mom had just found the Lord? Would her faith be strong enough to turn to Him for support or would her faith be too new and weak to sustain her, causing her to turn away? One question led to another, resulting in the story you hold in your hands.

This is my first published book and I would love to hear from my readers. You can reach me at diane@dianeburkeauthor.com. I will answer as quickly as possible.

I hope you enjoy *Midnight Caller.*

Diane Burke

QUESTIONS FOR DISCUSSION

1. As a child, Erin felt abandoned by her constantly working father and later in life she was deserted and betrayed by her husband. How did these experiences impact her adult life?

2. As a child, Erin was beaten and abused by her mother—so was the villain. How did child abuse impact their lives? What do you think made the difference between them as they chose opposite paths in their adult lives?

3. Erin's mother was an alcoholic. Alcoholism impacts an entire family, not just the person with the disease. Do you know anyone with this problem? How has this impacted their lives?

4. Erin is a strong, independent woman satisfied with the direction of her life. However, she comes to realize Tony fills an empty place in her life. What qualities draw her to him?

5. What draws Tony to Erin?

6. Erin had just found the Lord when she was forced to face significant trials in her life. Do you think her faith strengthened her? In your opinion, what forges a strong faith?

7. Tony was afraid to become a father because he knew the importance of the job and was afraid he'd fail. Do you think Tony demonstrated characteristics of a good dad?

Do you think it was brave of him to admit he was afraid of failure? Have you ever been afraid to fail? What did you do to overcome the fear?

8. Tony told Erin that God hears her prayers even if they are merely whispers in the dark. Have you ever wondered if God hears your prayers?

9. Erin was drawn to the biblical passage "Yea, though I walk through the valley of the shadow of death, I will fear no evil for Thou art with me." Do you believe God is always with us even in our hour of need? Do you have any examples in your own life?

10. God often puts people in our lives to help us when we need it the most. What roles did Tess and Patrick play that might make you think they were part of God's plan?

11. Is there anything in Erin's story that inspires you in your own life?

*When his niece unexpectedly arrives at his
Montana ranch, Jules Parrish has no idea what to do
with her—or with Olivia Rose, the pretty teacher
who brought her. Will they be able to build
a life—and family—together?*

*Here's a sneak peek of "Montana Rose"
by Cheryl St.John, one of the
touching stories in the new collection,
TO BE A MOTHER,
available April 2010
from Love Inspired® Historical.*

Jules Parrish squinted from beneath his hat brim, certain the waves of heat were playing with his eyes. Two females—one a woman, the other a child—stood as he approached.

The woman walked toward him. Jules dismounted and approached her. "What are you doing here?"

The woman stopped several feet away. "Mr. Parrish?"

"Yeah, who are you?"

"I'm Olivia Rose. I was an instructor at the Hedward Girls Academy." She glanced back over her shoulder at the girl who watched them. "My young charge is Emily Sadler, the daughter of Meriel Sadler."

She had his attention now. He hadn't heard his sister's name in years. *Meriel.*

"The academy was forced to close. I thought Emily should be with family. You're the only family she has, so I brought her to you."

He took off his hat and raked his fingers through dark, wavy hair. "Lady, I spend every waking hour working horses and cows. I sleep in a one-room cabin. I don't know anything about kids—and especially not girls."

"What do you suggest?"

"I don't know. All I know is, she can't stay here."

Will Olivia be able to change Jules's mind
and find a home for Emily—and herself?

Find out in
TO BE A MOTHER,
the heartwarming anthology from
Cheryl St.John and Ruth Axtell Morren,
available April 2010
only from Love Inspired® Historical.

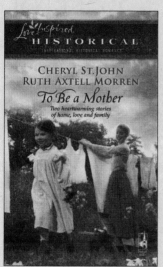

LARGER-PRINT BOOKS!

**GET 2 FREE
LARGER-PRINT NOVELS
PLUS 2 FREE
MYSTERY GIFTS**

Love Inspired
SUSPENSE
RIVETING INSPIRATIONAL ROMANCE

Larger-print novels are now available...

YES! Please send me 2 FREE LARGER-PRINT Love Inspired® Suspense novels and my 2 FREE mystery gifts (gifts are worth about $10). After receiving them, if I don't wish to receive any more books, I can return the shipping statement marked "cancel". If I don't cancel, I will receive 4 brand-new novels every month and be billed just $4.74 per book in the U.S. or $5.24 per book in Canada. That's a saving of over 20% off the cover price. It's quite a bargain! Shipping and handling is just 50¢ per book in the U.S. and 75¢ per book in Canada.* I understand that accepting the 2 free books and gifts places me under no obligation to buy anything. I can always return a shipment and cancel at any time. Even if I never buy another book, the two free books and gifts are mine to keep forever.

110 IDN E4AN 310 IDN E4AY

Name	(PLEASE PRINT)	
Address		Apt. #
City	State/Prov.	Zip/Postal Code

Signature (if under 18, a parent or guardian must sign)

Mail to **Steeple Hill Reader Service:**
IN U.S.A.: P.O. Box 1867, Buffalo, NY 14240-1867
IN CANADA: P.O. Box 609, Fort Erie, Ontario L2A 5X3

Not valid for current subscribers to Love Inspired Suspense larger-print books.

**Are you a current subscriber to Love Inspired Suspense books
and want to receive the larger-print edition?
Call 1-800-873-8635 or visit www.morefreebooks.com.**

* Terms and prices subject to change without notice. Prices do not include applicable taxes. Sales tax applicable in N.Y. Canadian residents will be charged applicable provincial taxes and GST. Offer not valid in Quebec. This offer is limited to one order per household. All orders subject to approval. Credit or debit balances in a customer's account(s) may be offset by any other outstanding balance owed by or to the customer. Please allow 4 to 6 weeks for delivery. Offer available while quantities last.

Your Privacy: Steeple Hill Books is committed to protecting your privacy. Our Privacy Policy is available online at www.SteepleHill.com or upon request from the Reader Service. From time to time we make our lists of customers available to reputable third parties who may have a product or service of interest to you. If you would prefer we not share your name and address, please check here. ☐

Help us get it right—We strive for accurate, respectful and relevant communications. To clarify or modify your communication preferences, visit us at www.ReaderService.com/consumerchoice.

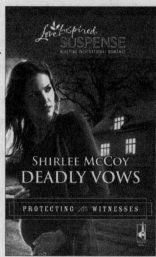